PROPAGANDA

A HISTORY OF PERSUASIVE ART IN THE GALAXY

STAR WARS™

PROPAGANDA

A HISTORY OF PERSUASIVE ART IN THE GALAXY

PABLO HIDALGO

HARPER
DESIGN

An Imprint of HarperCollinsPublishers

CONTENTS

PINNACLE OF FREEDOM, THE RESISTANCE

A GALAXY OF WAR AND ART

BY JANYOR OF BITH

Our galaxy has known war for ages. That such conflict is inevitable should encourage us to embrace the blessed islands of peace that dot the oceans of time. It is incumbent upon us to advance the best in civilization during these respites before the ravages of war drag us back into the ashes. Artistic expression is indeed among the best of what societies have to offer. But unlike other advancements that flourish solely in peacetime, art can be fueled by war.

Across the scattered civilizations of the galaxy, war and art are inextricably linked. Both forms of expression share similar origin points in a culture's time line. A people able to take moments away from frenzied survival to pick up a brush or shape some clay enjoys, at least, some modicum of stability. Predators and famine have been held at bay for the scraps of time and comfort required to create.

From this, we conclude that these primitives *have*. And to *have* is to be targeted by those who *covet*. So the brush and potter's wheel attract the sling and stone. War erupts, which spurs the artist to react. Bursts of violence and the rush of conquest stir the spirit. Art reflects the conflict at hand, and in turn, may spur the next one. The artist becomes an instrument of conflict, even if he or she rejects the conflict itself.

As an artist, I have worked in many forms and media in my fourteen decades of life, and have also witnessed more than my fill of war. These syncopated patterns of creativity and destruction are chronicled in my art, which serves as a type of diary during these tumultuous times. Each armed conflict sparked artistic comment, which in many cases fed further conflict by striking exposed nerves in damaged societies. That this pattern can be found in the infant steps of the earliest tribes, as well as in the galactic conflicts of the allegedly advanced, may be depressing to some. Is it not a scathing indictment that we, as sentients, are locked into an unbreakable cycle of destruction?

I am not so fatalistic, however. For in my time, I have witnessed breathtaking creation emerge from appalling destruction. Art and

LEFT: Latest work by Janyor of Bith, created on the eve of the Hosnian Cataclysm. **ABOVE:** Janyor of Bith, holo by Adree-515.

Early Imperial unity poster by Janyor of Bith, created after the drafting of the Imperial Charter. In his autobiocron *Dear Anguillon,* Janyor described his disgust with himself upon reflecting on this unflinching fascist image, complete with brutalist Atrisian Basic motto "Empire united over all."

war are inevitable, yes, but they are also forges that can temper souls unlike any other. The worst of us is required to draw out the best of us.

An artist need not be a soldier to be a warrior (although I've been both, I hesitate to say). In turbulent times, an artist uses expression and symbolism as weapons, transforming art into propaganda. There are scholars of art who reserve only the most scornful tones to utter that word. I am not one of them. Art is a reflection of civilization. So is war. Art in the service of war is doubly so. To dismiss propaganda as a lesser form of art is to deny a fundamental part of who we are. The fact that the Coalition for the Preservation of the New Order was the patron behind Dalraga de Cueravon's *Imperius Unitada ober Totallex* does not strip away the artist's merits, not without descending a slope of unreasonable demands for artistic integrity. Can a patriot never touch a canvas?

I have been a propagandist, a young defender of the Republic, blind to its faults and gripped by a jingoist's fervor to support the soldiers of the Clone Wars. I believed in the rhetoric of Chancellor Palpatine. I believed in the evils of Count Dooku and the selfish damage inflicted by the Separatist Alliance. I believed in the promise of a thousand years of peace and thought the Galactic Empire was just what civilization needed: a strong guiding hand to keep us on a path to a bright future.

That future was not to be. I was not shy to express my disillusionment with the so-called New Order. The protest art pieces that resulted were full of blunt anger and inarticulate condemnation of the Galactic Empire's excesses and, in time, they forced me into exile. There I gained new artistic currency among the elites who valued such things. My eyes had been opened (an odd metaphor for a lidless Bith to employ, but here we are), yet I was still a propagandist. This time, I was doing my part for the burgeoning Alliance to Restore the Republic. I had a new patron, one that aligned with my rebellious heart.

The Rebel Alliance was perennially underequipped to battle the Empire. Its meager resources could in no way compare to the vast might of the Imperial war machine. But to the Rebellion, a well-crafted message of hope and defiance could mean more than ten thousand blaster rifles, a thousand starfighters, or a hundred capital ships. The Galactic Civil War was not a battle for territory. It was a struggle for the hearts and minds of the galaxy. The war artist was the Rebel Alliance's superweapon.

In the rickety Alliance government that rose in the wake of the Galactic Civil War, I ascended to a rank of Propaganda Bureau Chief. With a small team of ostracized illustrators, beleaguered journalists, and other such willful idealists, we crafted messages meant to explain to the citizenry of the galaxy the *true* state of the Empire. In practice, it meant attempting to counter the nonstop Imperial propaganda spewed into the ether by a government with nigh endless resources. I admit, to tip back the scales upset by its outrageous lies, we were forced to craft lies of our own and hope that somewhere in the balance a truth could be found.

In the years that followed the destruction of the second Death Star, and the capitulation of the Imperial military, I fooled myself into thinking the propagandist's brush would grow dry and brittle. I retired to enjoy my island of peace, becoming soft and complacent in the cosmopolitan core. My vigilant eyes grew cloudy with cataracts of comfort and largesse. My fires of outrage cooled while I received accolades and made speeches at burnished assembly halls.

I was the kind of old, blind fool that infuriates young artists who create with fire in their bellies. Thankfully, this new generation was eager to speak, and the New Republic allowed for such expression. They warned against the treaties of convenience that kept the former Empire at arm's length and away from prying eyes. They warned that the New Republic was becoming too lax in its effort to avoid any whiffs of autocracy. They warned that the titans of commerce were happy to bend export restrictions and help fuel the secret militarization in First Order territory.

We, the old fools, did not heed such augury. These new artists told us that the First Order was the reincarnation of an old evil and that the lethargy and corruption of the New Republic were accomplices. Thankfully, a Resistance of the young has emerged, and artists stand amid its ranks. I regret that it required an unmistakable provocation of violence to awaken me from my slumber. Years of inflated reflection on the past failed to translate experience into action until it was too late.

Today, as I write this, the cinders of the Hosnian system still glow. The First Order has struck from its hidden grounds on the far side of the galaxy and, in a single blow, has undone decades of growth and healing from the last great war. Thus the conflict begins anew.

The Bith have no tears, but I know their meaning. My brushes are wet with tears, ready to paint the sobs of yet another generation. My hand may be frail, but I am determined to make penance for my failure to recognize the recurrent chain of events, which shackles the galaxy. I am once more a propagandist, for I am too old to fight in any other way.

There are lessons to be learned, my fellow student, from the succession of conflict and creativity that has repeated itself since time immemorial. Understand this chain and understand your part in it, and you will better know when it is time to repeat it and time to break it.

Janyor of Bith
Cressdelta Coven
North Hoostra, Garel

Janyor of Bith is a renowned painter, poet, and sculptor from Garel. He is the four-time recipient of the Xephi Sep Award, served as poet laureate for Clak'dor VII, and is professor emeritus of the Kime Enanrum Academy of Arts on Coruscant. He famously sculpted the Bail Organa dedicatory statue of the New Republic that, until recently, stood in the Senate Square of Hosnian Prime.

PART I:
THE REPUBLIC

THE LAST
ERA OF PEACE

During the height of the Galactic Republic, the specter of widespread warfare had been forgotten. A full-scale war had not rocked the galaxy in centuries. The last great conflict, having been waged for the soul of civilization itself, was a decisive war fought between the Jedi Order and the Sith Lords. The Republic victory was so definitive that it reinvented itself, resettling its capital on Coruscant after a devastating ouster. History reset its chrono on this date, and from that moment, the modern Galactic Republic was born. Societal memories and official calendars started fresh, and the time before this rebirth was

forgotten as a dark age, lumped into a collective whole known as the "Old Republic."

That is not to say that there weren't isolated conflicts in this new era. With any society, there are failures of diplomacy and communication that can be resolved only with cannon and carnage. These were blessedly few, and many were quelled in their earliest stages by the earnest pursuit of peace by the Jedi Order. Jedi negotiators settled disputes before they inflamed war. The Jedi Code itself evolved to include provisions that would keep the Jedi Knights apart from such conflicts. The Jedi were keepers

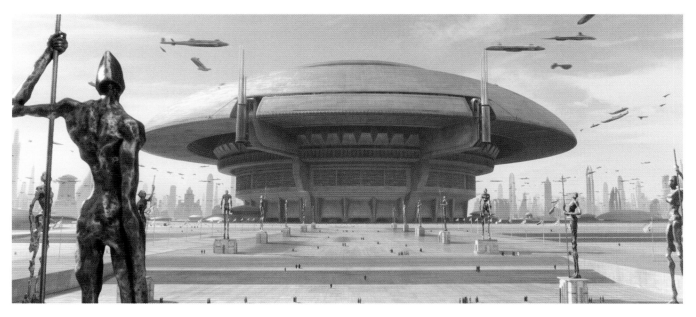

Lined with stylized depictions of ancient humanoids, the Avenue of the Core Founders is a broad promenade leading to the massive Senate rotunda. The sundrenched concourse, at a rarified plateau atop the stacked levels of the megacity, was often presented as the visualized ideal of Republic sophistication.

The simpler times of peace in the Republic allowed for leisure activities to achieve galactic attention. The Boonta Eve Podrace, though based beyond the Republic's borders in the independent Outer Rim, garnered coverage and attention even in the Core Worlds.

of the peace, not soldiers. As such, Jedi were rarely viewed as warriors, and their faces did not adorn messages of propaganda.

The government artwork of this time was largely about preserving the status quo. Peace was good for commerce; as such, the art beautified the distractions that member worlds offered in the name of lucrative tourism. Worlds with rich cultures, like Naboo, broadcast their histories to neighboring planets. Even far-flung worlds with shady reputations like Tatooine tried cleaning up their image to attract visitors for such events as the Boonta Eve Classic. During the Chancellery of Finis Valorum, initial work began on millennial celebrations that would have marked the thousand-year anniversary of the Republic's foundation. Such exploration of logo designs and artwork now stand as an ironic artifact of a myopic regime, since the Republic dissolved before any such milestone could be reached.

The titans of business, like the massive Trade Federation, funneled vast amounts of their limitless capital into spreading the word of their essential services to the galaxy. They attempted to foster goodwill and influence in the Republic to detract from their legally questionable practices in the less patrolled regions of the galaxy. Their propaganda was part of a vast brand-building effort to ensure a steady flow of profits reaped on the backs of the unfortunate.

Appealing to the comfortable by-products of avarice proved effective for such entities as the Trade Federation, the Commerce Guild, and the Corporate Alliance. But outsider artists objected and made their disagreements visible in select but well-publicized outbursts of anti-corporate propaganda. Such deep-pocketed enterprises as the InterGalactic Banking Clan could paper over any protest with only a fraction of the interest earned on their troves. In cases where an outraged artist proved particularly obstinate, these corporate barons could use force—droid soldiers and garrulous lawyers were armed to make troublesome artists disappear.

In contrast, institutions like the Jedi Order did little to cultivate their image or build their mindshare of the Republic's populace, relying instead on historic precedent. This proved a difficult proposition, as the galaxy strongly favored looking to the future rather than the past.

With eyes toward expansion into the uncharted reaches of the Outer Rim, the traditions of the Core became passé. Opportunity beckoned from beyond the borders of the Mid Rim worlds. The congested planets of the interior were saturated with messages of promise lying outward, a reversal from long-held notions that Coruscant represented the icon of advancement. Republic wordsmiths and artists collaborated to create a sense of civic duty, of manifest destiny, and of deep obligation to spread the Republic banner from Rim to Rim.

For the well-settled and wealthy elite of the galaxy's most crowded centers, such notions were quaint but uninspiring. It was the citizens of the Inner Rim, those who had been crowded out of opportunity in the Core, who answered the call for new life in the frontier of the Outer Rim. The Core Worlders became more enamored with the fleeting distractions of fame and fashion, transitory fascinations with sophistication that left little room for messages of faith or tradition that the Jedi exemplified. The lack of representation in the galactic mindshare undoubtedly fixed their future, as dark forces were on the rise that would poison the public sentiment toward the Jedi in the decades to come.

The OUTER RIM

BEGIN AGAIN IN A GOLDEN LAND OF OPPORTUNITY!

Republic incentives for the brave and hardy! New colonies and adventures await!

SETTLE THE OUTER RIM
Artist Unknown (Eleven Star Marketing)

Deep space imagery meant to evoke adventurism and mystery was common in the Eleven Star Marketing's campaign launched on behalf of the Republic Ministry of Economic Development. Even the most superficial digging into corporate relations will uncover that Eleven Star, based out of Cato Neimoidia, was also the public relations agency for the Trade Federation. The wanderlust-stricken souls stirred into action by these messages would be guided toward Trade Federation–controlled hyperspace routes with corresponding tariffs and registration fees. Such lucrative administrative overlap was frequently cited as "inevitable," particularly by the Republic politicians who met with Federation lobbyists to ensure said inevitability would occur.

TAXATION WITHOUT FEDERATION
Ganamey Davloterra

Originally commissioned as a Core-edition insert in a HoloNet News weekend issue, this striking piece spread throughout the Mid Rim as unauthorized reproductions transmitted via personal infocache nodes as well as physically printed adverslicks. The taxation of trade routes was a thorn in the side of the Senate as it attempted to curtail the massive influence of the Trade Federation. However, Neimoidian spin doctors painted this and other protest imagery as a blatantly racist campaign. The fat Neimoidian pluto-crat was a popular stereotype, and this piece bolstered it with unfortunate overtones of duplicity and rapaciousness.

SAFE IN OUR HANDS
Nute Gunray (concept); Artist Unknown (Eleven Star Marketing)

The Neimoidian language has no word for "nurturing." The concept seems absent from the species' psychology. Early Neimoidian development is a cutthroat competition for food and attention, as near-helpless devel-oping Neimoidians clamber for dominance and survival. Therefore, this advertisement's attempt—said to be authored by Viceroy Nute Gunray himself—to convey stability and guidance cannot help but be colored with underlying images of strength, dominance, and quite literally, underhanded manipula-tion. Some saw it as Gunray's dream made clear—to own all of Coruscant as yet another shining bauble in a collection of misbegot-ten gems. Under Gunray's tenure, the Trade Federation would loudly counter such claims as common anti-Niemoidian prejudice.

SAFE

IN OUR HANDS

Working hand in hand with their colleagues in the Galactic Senate, the dedicated members of the Trade Federation strive to bring their message of peace, security and prosperity to every arm of the galaxy.

THE TRADE FEDERATION

FEDERATION PROFITS = GALACTIC POVERTY

VOTE YES ON PROP 31-814D
TAX FREE TRADE ZONES

◁

VOTE YES ON PROP 31-814D
Artist Unknown

Anti–Trade Federation protestors refocused their rhetoric in future messages and images, keeping depictions of the Neimoidians out of their artwork to avoid confusing matters with cultural insensitivities. Their tactic favored simple messaging meant to cut through the obfuscation favored by Trade Federation lobbyists, and simplified the argument to the most universal bottom line: money. The inefficiencies in the Republic led to insufficient funds to cover the most prized of services. Why shouldn't the corporations pull their weight?

▷

INVEST WISELY
Rush Clovis (concept); Tantagru Motts-Danel (execution)

The InterGalactic Banking Clan likewise had an image problem during the last days of the Republic. Despite the best efforts of several highly placed executives on its board, the ruling Core Five (composed entirely of Muuns) simply never understood the need to cultivate trust and stability in their messaging. To these reclusive, statuesque beings cloistered in the snow-swept peaks of their native Scipio, the dominance of Muuns over galactic finances was simply a given. The Muuns had kept the credits flowing since the earliest, darkest days of interstellar exploration, and so it should continue uninterrupted into the future. Creatively compromised communications campaigns became an unsuccessful mix of metaphors, Muun iconography, and Banking Clan hardware with words of encouragement that seem distant and disconnected.

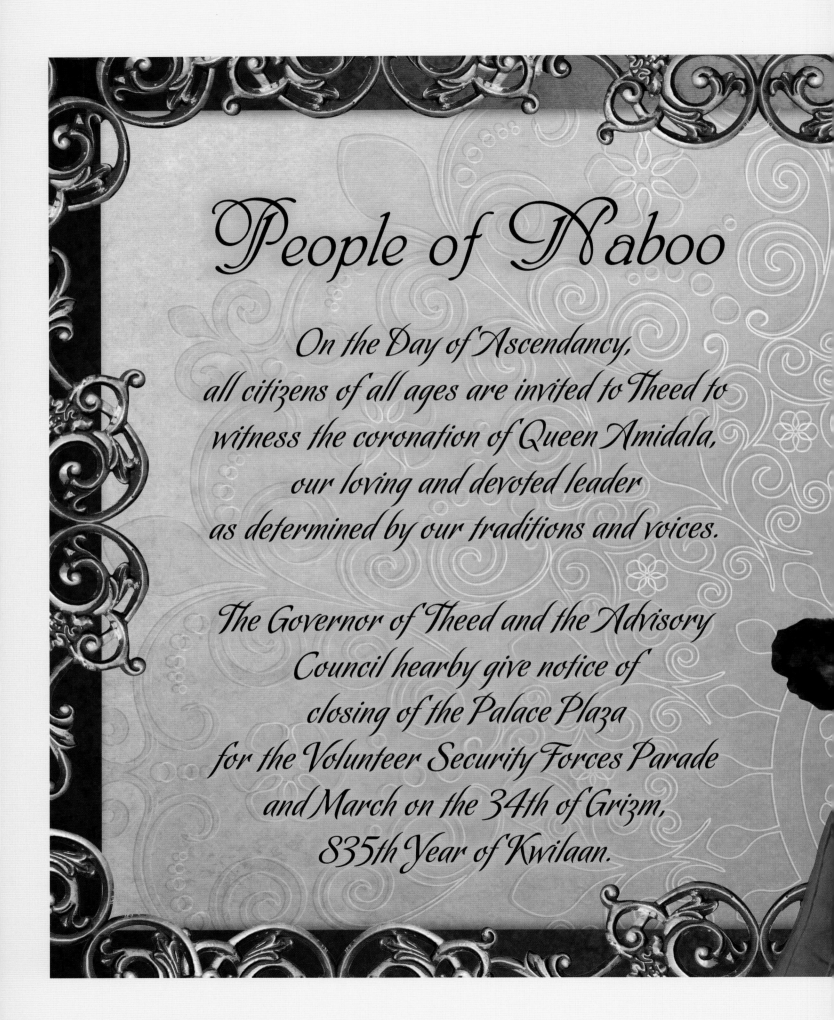

People of Naboo

On the Day of Ascendancy,
all citizens of all ages are invited to Theed to
witness the coronation of Queen Amidala,
our loving and devoted leader
as determined by our traditions and voices.

The Governor of Theed and the Advisory
Council hearby give notice of
closing of the Palace Plaza
for the Volunteer Security Forces Parade
and March on the 34th of Grizm,
835th Year of Kwilaan.

NABOO CORONATION
Palo Jemabie

When historians look back at the Republic with a sense of longing for artistic elegance and refinement, they often cite Naboo as the idolized zenith of cultural sophistication. Every act carried out by the Naboo people, whether a lowly laborer or a royal courtier, is steeped in tradition and adorned with symbols. Theirs is a culture that takes pains to protect their traditions and keep impersonal modernity out of their daily lives. This may make the Naboo people seem odd or off-putting to others, and has long been a source of contention between the colonists and the native Gungans.

Naboo saw the coronation of Queen Amidala as the ultimate expression of cherished values. Amidala was not the youngest queen ever elected, but at age fourteen, she was certainly the youngest in centuries. The notion of electing so young a monarch underscored the emphasis the Naboo people placed on educating children, and their desire to keep cynical manipulators of the type tempered by decades in politics out of their local government.

1000 YEARS
PEACE
Supreme Chancellor of the Republic, Finis Valorum,
along with the distinguished members of Galactic Senate,
cordially invite you and your loved ones to share in a grand celebration
commemorating a millenium of peace.

MILLENNIAL CELEBRATION INVITATION

Naveela Betuine (concept and layout);
Dashira Dobeq (final execution)

A near-final representation of the millennial invitation that had undergone no less than 250 revisions by Chancellor Finis Valorum, this piece ultimately never saw distribution. Concerned with his deteriorating public image, Valorum rejected earlier iterations for being too cold, too warm, too exclusive, or too directionless. Such indecision was a common characteristic of Valorum's final months in office. Ultimately, the Chancellor delegated such design decisions to his friend and supporter, Senator Sheev Palpatine of Naboo, who recommended this design. The central figure is Sistros, an ancient lawgiver that helped set the original constitution of the post-Sith Galactic Republic in order. Palpatine suggested the icon as a binding representation of the galactic multitudes, whose faceless aspect could act as a cipher for the many humanoids in the galaxy.

THE SPORT'S GREATEST RIVALRY

Codenka Mafurias

Before the outbreak of war, the twilight of the Republic was an era of distractions, with citizens from all walks of life following escapist pursuits. Historians rebuke the people of this last age for being taken in by such circuses when their attentions should have been focused on the malfeasances and corruption in the Senate and other governing institutions. But events like the professional podrace circuit sold pre-packaged narratives that spoke to the intrinsic need of stories: tales of heroes and villains pitted against each other in arenas of escalating complications. Had Codenka Mafurias, a talented illustrator from Malastare, been able to describe the dramas of politics with the deft hand she displays in this piece that pits underdog Ben Quadinaros against arch-rival Sebulba, perhaps more people would have been invested in the coming collapse of comfortable civilization as we knew it.

A GALAXY DIVIDED

The Galactic Republic was the Republic of legend, greater than distance or time. Tales of its founding have been occluded by the haze of the intervening millennia, and its rebirth a thousand years ago was regarded as its latest evolution in an unending cycle. Like the greatest of trees, however, the Republic's decline began from within, with a deep rot that was not apparent until it was too late.

Many galactic senators and lawmakers lived their lives within the opulence of Coruscant's towering cities. They grew increasingly distant from their representative worlds and were more responsive to the lucre promised by corporate interests than the pleas of their constituents. In this way, essential services to the outlying worlds of the Republic began to fail. Many worlds questioned if the increasing burden of taxation was worth such paltry representation.

Chancellor Sheev Palpatine of Naboo was elected on a groundswell of sympathy for his homeworld, which had been subjected to a cruel blockade by the Trade Federation. The blockade was an outrageous overstepping of boundaries by a corporation attempting to find loopholes in an inconvenient tax code. It resulted in the brief, but historic, Battle of Naboo that had the Trade Federation

"It is with great reluctance that I have agreed to this calling," Chancellor Sheev Palpatine told the assembled Senate upon being granted Emergency Powers in a time of crisis. The clarity of hindsight cast these words in a far different light.

on the losing side. The corporation's leader, Viceroy Nute Gunray, was arrested by the Republic. But his highly placed allies in the courts arranged for mistrial after mistrial, and Gunray escaped legal repercussions.

The disaffected in the galaxy decried the mistrials as an appalling example of corruption. Even with a personal stake in seeing justice served to Gunray, the Supreme Chancellor could not keep the courts from being swayed. More and more systems demanded accountability on Coruscant, but these voices were scattered and disorganized.

Enter Count Dooku. Head of the noble house of Serenno, Dooku emerged as a charismatic firebrand who laid bare the inequities of the Republic. He encouraged worlds to tender articles of secession from the Republic, spurring a tide of separatism that spread across the Republic. Dooku had a commanding voice that demanded attention. He also had the authority inherited from his previous role, a former Jedi Master of the Order. Once again, the Jedi Order's eschewing of the galactic spotlight allowed another to reshape the image of the Jedi, and for nearly a decade, the most famous Jedi in the galaxy was one who advocated for the dissolution of the Republic.

Among the growing members of the Separatist Alliance were artists who held back little in complaining about the sins of the Core. Countless messages of corruption were broadcast to worlds on the borderlands, systems that never realized there was an alternative to the Republic. Serenno, Raxus, Onderon, Ando, Sullust, Umbara, and other major worlds seceded, taking with them their resources and tax revenue.

Coruscant was in a panic. Multiple agencies within the government and those contracted from the private sector were tasked with taking the reins of an out-of-control narrative. Rather than be tarred with the epithet *ineffectual* that colored Chancellor Valorum's legacy, Palpatine was recast as a beleaguered patriot doing his best to root out corruption from a complacent system. While such messaging did not stem the tide of separatism, it did allow for Palpatine to accrue more executive powers and extend his term beyond constitutional limitations to better deal with the growing crisis.

In a darkened conference room in the Geonosian foundries, Count Dooku forges an insidious pact with corporate barons and weapons designers to arm and fund the Separatist Alliance.

and quickly painted the Separatists as anarchists. The Separatists countered by reminding the galaxy that Coruscant simply did not know what was best for the galaxy.

The increasing debt and dwindling taxation revenue caused the Republic's economy to falter. Action was needed to bring the Separatists in line. The Separatist rhetoric grew more aggressive. Several worlds activated long-dormant or purely ceremonial armed forces in displays of armed independence.

Within the halls of government, the unthinkable was discussed: open warfare. The Republic had no standing army, so representatives within the Senate proposed the Military Creation Act. Euphemistically described as a preventative exploration of logistics, the Act called for unifying the member worlds of the Republic to define a galactic military force. Some in the Senate saw it as the saber rattling needed to cow the Separatists into submission. Others saw it as an inevitable prelude to war. Even worlds loyal to the Republic were divided by the Act. Naboo and Alderaan were most notably against the Military Creation Act, while other worlds like Carida and Eriadu enthusiastically championed it.

It is no small irony that the Act itself was superfluous. War came before it was ever voted upon, and the strange eddies of fate gifted the Republic with a clone army, ready to use—a gift from a secret Jedi mission launched a decade earlier.

The Clone Wars had begun.

For a decade—two and a half terms—of Palpatine's Chancellery, the struggle for the future was in the hearts and minds of the citizens. Separatist propagandists expounded on the romanticized benefits of self-determination, liberty, and independence. Republic campaigns, on the other hand, lauded strength through unity. When flash points of violence marred the ongoing political discourse, the Republic seized on the narrative of law and order

Vast open spaces on the upper levels of Coruscant are hastily transformed into military staging grounds. The first generation of clone troopers arrive at the capital for organization and deployment as the Grand Army of the Republic.

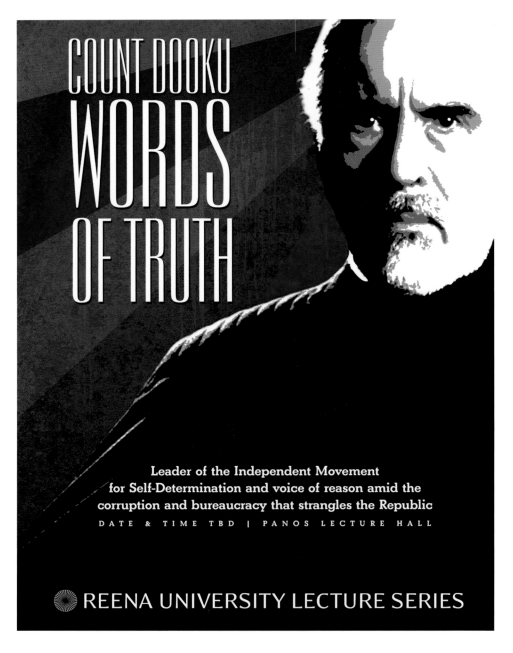

COUNT DOOKU: WORDS OF TRUTH

Ansibella Dellu

Count Dooku's words of inflammatory rhetoric found an audience among the young intellectuals of Inner and Mid Rim universities. The charismatic Separatist and former Jedi used his experience operating within the corridors of the Galactic Republic to damn the government for its hypocrisies, corruption, and ineffectiveness. Dooku exuded confidence and authority, but expounded a message of rebellion that mesmerized young psyches and spurred them to action. As the Separatist crisis became more and more heated, Dooku's appearances grew rarer and came together with much shorter notice. This rare specimen of a work-in-progress poster by Ansibella Dellu during her university years survived the loyalty purges enacted by the Imperial Security Bureau following the conclusion of the Clone Wars.

2,000 SENATORS

Kas unloDos

Mid Rim worlds were a hotbed of secessionist talk during the Separatist crisis that precipitated the conflagration of the Clone Wars. The so-called jumpover sectors of the Republic lacked the political pull of the central systems or the economic exploitation opportunities that lay in the Outer Rim. On the fertile plains of Ukio, Count Dooku's fiery separatist rhetoric found purchase. The agrarian world began to question what value was reciprocated for being the breadbasket to the Core Worlds. After citing a litany of neglect from Coruscant, the Senatorial representatives of the Abrion sector (which included Ukio) tendered their articles of secession. A Ukian artist, Kas unloDos, captured the sentiment common among her people—that the Republic was distant, dispassionate, and not worth the membership.

THERE ARE 2000 SENATORS INSIDE THIS BUILDING

NONE OF THEM CARE ABOUT YOU

CONFEDERACY OF INDEPENDENT SYSTEMS

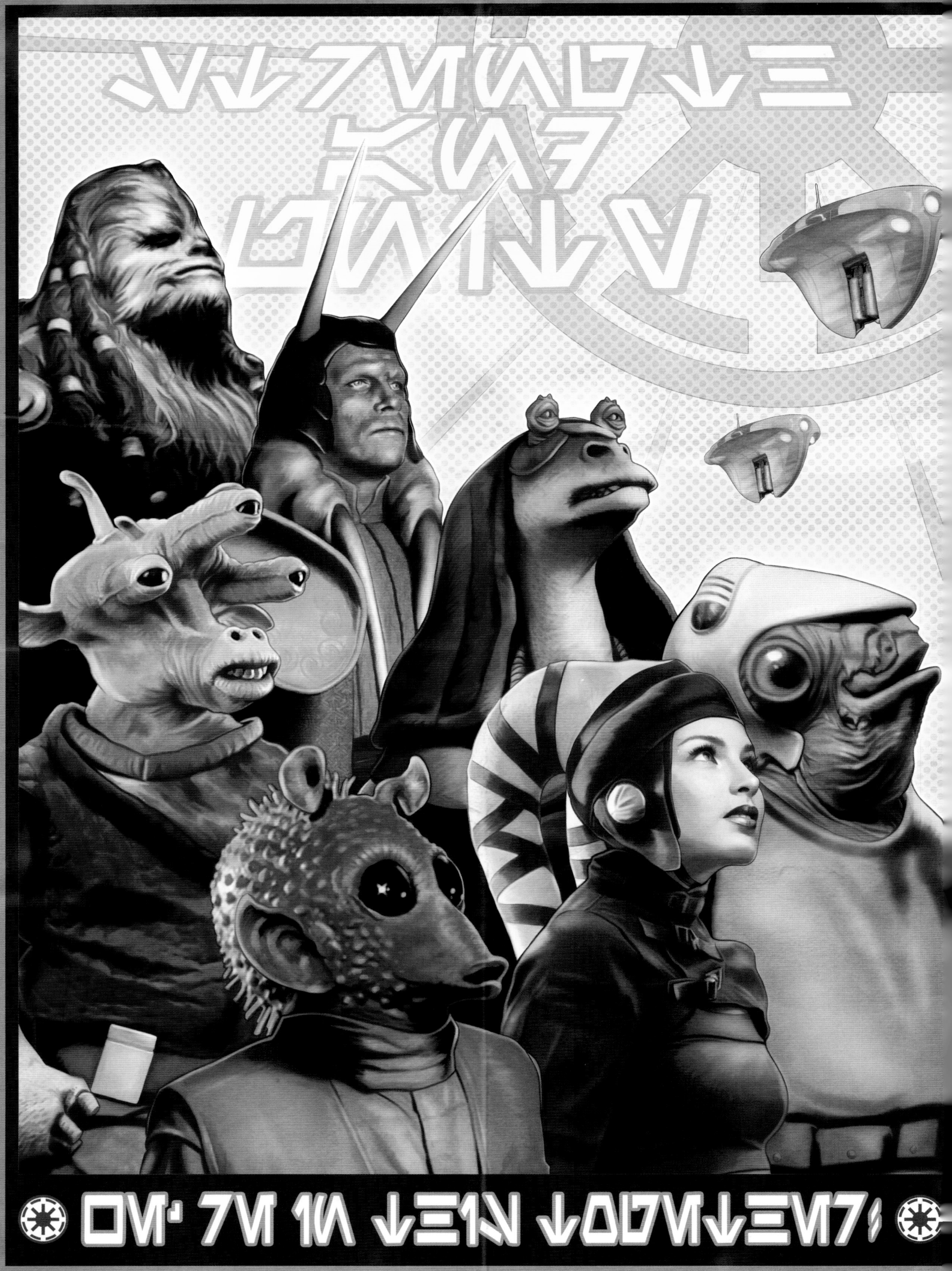

STRENGTH AND UNITY

Mas Amedda (concept); Angilar Bosh (execution)

Supreme Chancellor Palpatine's Loyalist Committee spearheaded attempts to stir patriotic unity in a rapidly splintering Republic. Vice Chancellor Mas Amedda proposed combating the human-dominated imagery of most Core-originated messaging with a campaign that presented the multicultural mosaic that made up the Republic worlds. It is no accident that the beings in this poster include representatives of worlds beyond the Core, with the Outer Rim cultures (Rodian, Twi'lek, and Mon Calamari) in the forefront, next to Mid Rim, Inner Rim, and Expansion Region denizens. Unfortunately for Amedda, the holonews outlets did not report on the assembled diversity in this image and instead chose to focus on the Vice Chancellor's self-inclusion. It is Amedda standing as the lone Chagrian in this poster, which became the subject of Core World talk-circuit ridicule. The words most associated with this campaign image in the media became *ego*, *narcissism*, and worse.

POLITICAL DOUBLETALK
Santos Bel-Pak

The Military Creation Act further polarized an already contentious debate about separatism. Nuance and inference fell by the wayside as the Act and the vote to make it real took shape. Once a date for the Military Creation Act vote was set, postponed, reset, and postponed again, the messaging on either side of the debate escalated in gravitas. A death's head superimposed on Chancellor Palpatine's visage left little doubt as to the intent of the message, but the copy bludgeons the point home. The United Committee for Galactic Peace was later discovered to be a front for the Roshu Sune, a radical splinter group of the Gotal Assembly for Separation proven to be behind a terrorist bombing campaign in the final months before the eruption of the Clone Wars.

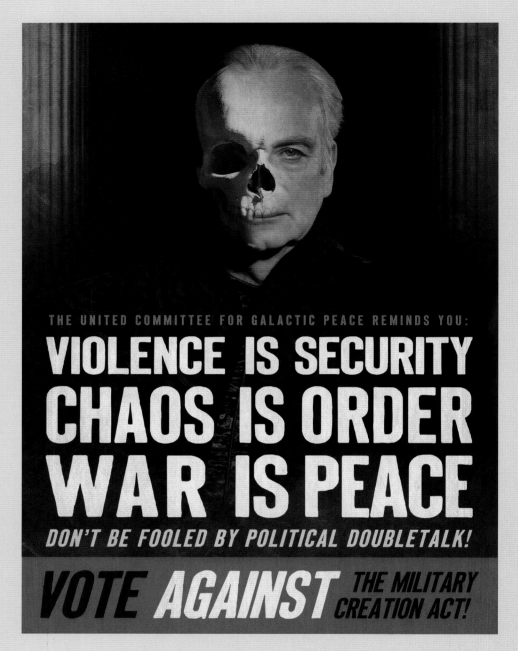

THE UNITED COMMITTEE FOR GALACTIC PEACE REMINDS YOU:
VIOLENCE IS SECURITY
CHAOS IS ORDER
WAR IS PEACE
DON'T BE FOOLED BY POLITICAL DOUBLETALK!

VOTE AGAINST THE MILITARY CREATION ACT!

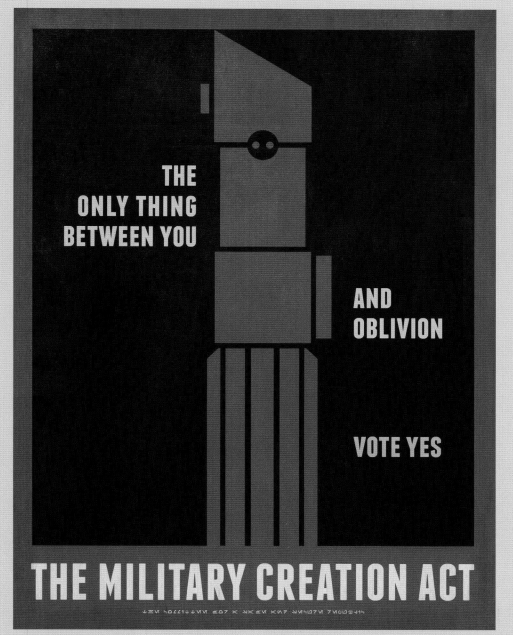

THE
ONLY THING
BETWEEN YOU

AND
OBLIVION

VOTE YES

THE MILITARY CREATION ACT

THE MILITARY CREATION ACT
Sannab Ro

To vividly counter the increasingly elabo-
rate anti-military messages propagated by
Separatist worlds, this particular example
of a Republic message endorsing the Military Creation Act uses sparse—some would
say stark—clarity. Intended for the Core
Worlds, it shows a graphic sophistication
that was in vogue at the time. Rather than
detail the inevitable horrors of impending
war, its singular lightsaber and well-chosen
words instead demonstrate how undefended
the Republic was. In crafting this message of
vulnerability, the Commission for a Safe and
Secure Republic (a nonprofit think tank based
on Level 5121, Coruscant) also unwittingly
seeded a secondary story that would grow
during the Clone Wars—that no salvation
lay in the direction of the Jedi Knights.

PART II:
THE CLONE WARS

LIKE FIRE ACROSS THE GALAXY

In the blink of an eye, it seemed, the galaxy was embroiled in a full-scale galactic war. The Separatist Alliance congealed into the Confederacy of Independent Systems, a coalition of loosely aligned worlds united for war. It pooled its resources to purchase huge quantities of battle droids, creating a ready-to-deploy army. The Republic mobilized its newly activated clone forces and hurriedly brevetted the Knights of the Jedi Order into military commanders. After a massive engagement on the distant world of Geonosis, a planet beyond the Republic borders, war was once again a reality in the galaxy.

The sudden mining of hyperspace routes allowed the Separatists to encircle the Republic as the next stage of the conflict began. To better navigate past the cordon, the Republic struck up an alliance with the reigning Hutt kajidics of the Outer Rim Territories. War made strange bedfellows—a few decades before, the Republic's Judiciary branch had launched a major public awareness campaign based on the threat posed by Hutt criminal activities. Such concerns were conveniently swept away when the Clone Wars turned the Hutts into allies, and the Hutts, as fit their nature, profited handsomely from such arrangements.

History tells us now that the greatest benefactors of the conflict were the corporations that funded the battle on both sides. The Trade Federation, the Corporate Alliance, the Commerce Guild, the Techno Union, and the InterGalactic Banking Clan made noises about Republic loyalty (or at least staunch neutrality) all the while cutting deals with the Separatists for conquered land

The Clone Wars did the unthinkable—it put the Core Worlds at risk. The insulated heart of the Republic had grown complacent in a sense of security and comfort. By war's end, the encroaching fear of Separatist attack reshaped the galaxy.

In this climate of dread and insecurity, Supreme Chancellor Palpatine promised reform. The Senate increasingly relinquished executive powers to him and his personally appointed advisors to better wage galactic war. This ceding of power culminated in Palpatine laying the blame for the carnage at the feet of the Jedi Order and its fellow conspirators in the Senate.

and assets. These corporations sold weapons and matériel to both sides of the war. When such treacherous collusion was exposed to Republic and Separatist citizens alike, artists amplified their efforts to vilify the rich titans of industry and commerce.

For the Republic, the war effort required a complex and far-reaching public support campaign to stir patriotism on the home front. Republic citizens were asked to buy war bonds, ration supplies, and curtail freedoms during this time of crisis. Chancellor Palpatine was routinely portrayed as a fatherly figure requiring help from his vast family to defend the Republic. Such an image made it easier to pass the emergency measures that gave Palpatine increased executive powers.

During the conflict, former independent states were challenged and courted by both sides in a bid to bolster resources and military strength. The Duchess Satine Kryze of Mandalore headed up a Council of Neutral Systems, more than 1,500 star systems that wanted no part in the war. Mandalore, home to many gifted artists, produced several works chastising both sides of the conflict while encouraging worlds to seek out true independence. However, these efforts faltered when Mandalore succumbed to its own internal conflict, and Satine Kryze was murdered by the shadowy forces of the Death Watch, a violent Mandalorian splinter group.

In Republic space, Count Dooku was branded as public enemy number one. The next greatest threat to Republic safety was General Grievous, the cyborg commander of the droid army. The Republic painted Grievous as a mechanical monstrosity—a description that played to deep-seated fears regarding droids. One by-product of the Clone Wars was an exacerbation of anti-droid sentiment in the galaxy. Once-useful automatons were branded as potential security threats, and combat droids were heavily regulated in Republic space.

The clone troopers, by contrast, were celebrated as heroes. Many Republic bulletins lauded the bravery of the "boys in white," and

Republic citizens were honored to billet clone troopers in their home during extended campaigns. The Kaminoans responsible for the creation of the clones were fast-tracked into Republic membership and given full Senatorial representation as a result of their industry. The need to keep clone supplies replenished caused a major reorganization of finances in the Republic, culminating in Supreme Chancellor Palpatine nationalizing the InterGalactic Banking Clan.

Absent from this hero-making were the Jedi Knights. Citizens who witnessed the Jedi in action were understandably in awe of their abilities, but it was the clone trooper who was the public face of the war effort. The mystic Jedi remained forever inscrutable to the Republic citizenry at large. To the Separatists, they were branded as hypocrites (thanks to firsthand criticism by Count Dooku). That they could so callously brandish a clone army—"slaves bred for war," as Separatist propaganda proclaimed—did not speak well to their character, though few among the Separatists knew that the Jedi were given no choice in the matter.

After three long years of conflict, which included military strikes that reached the heart of the Core Worlds, public opinion soured on the war. More and more citizens saw the conflict as fruitless and demanded a negotiated settlement. It was during the height of this discontent that Chancellor Palpatine shocked the galaxy by exposing the Jedi Order as traitors. Despite some muted protests in the Senate, Palpatine easily spread this claim by reminding the galaxy that Dooku, the Republic's greatest threat in a thousand years, was a former Jedi. When the Republic military destroyed both Count Dooku and General Grievous, the war was brought to an end.

To ensure such a war would never happen again, Palpatine re-formed the Republic as the First Galactic Empire. A war-weary galaxy was more than ready to erase the Jedi Order from the pages of history and turned instead to the battle-tested Imperial war machine for its salvation from chaos.

◁

JEDI UNITE FOR PEACE
Byno Doubton, COMPOR

The back-to-back discovery of a clone army secretly commissioned by a former Jedi Master, and the Separatist Alliance ready for war, left the Jedi Order with no choice but to abandon its traditional role of negotiators and peacekeepers and to take up arms. As the Republic's most seasoned combatants, Jedi Knights were given the rank of generals over the newly formed Grand Army of the Republic. The Jedi Council expressed its reservations about this new function, but nonetheless it was committed in its duty to the Senate. It was Chancellor Palpatine himself who recommended that images such as this poster not be used to bolster wartime support for the Republic, citing sympathy toward the Jedi discomfort. Very few examples exist of government-approved imagery that showcased the Jedi Knights in their capacity as military leaders.

▷

UNITE
Byno Doubton, COMPOR

The next iteration of the unity communications campaign exchanged lightsabers for clone troopers. The polished white armor of the Grand Army infantry would become the signature icon of the conflict that quickly took its name from these very ranks: the Clone Wars. The Commission for the Preservation of the Republic (COMPOR) worked closely with the newly formed Republic War Office to transform the clone trooper into the poster boy of patriotic messages across the galaxy. The ancient eight-spoked sigil of the Republic found new application on freshly minted Republic war machinery as well as on snapping flags and military banners. These were the soldiers risking all for the sanctity of the Republic and the cherished freedoms of democracy—so went the stirring messages, ballads, and holographic short subjects. Absent from these portrayals was any lingering focus on the Jedi Order.

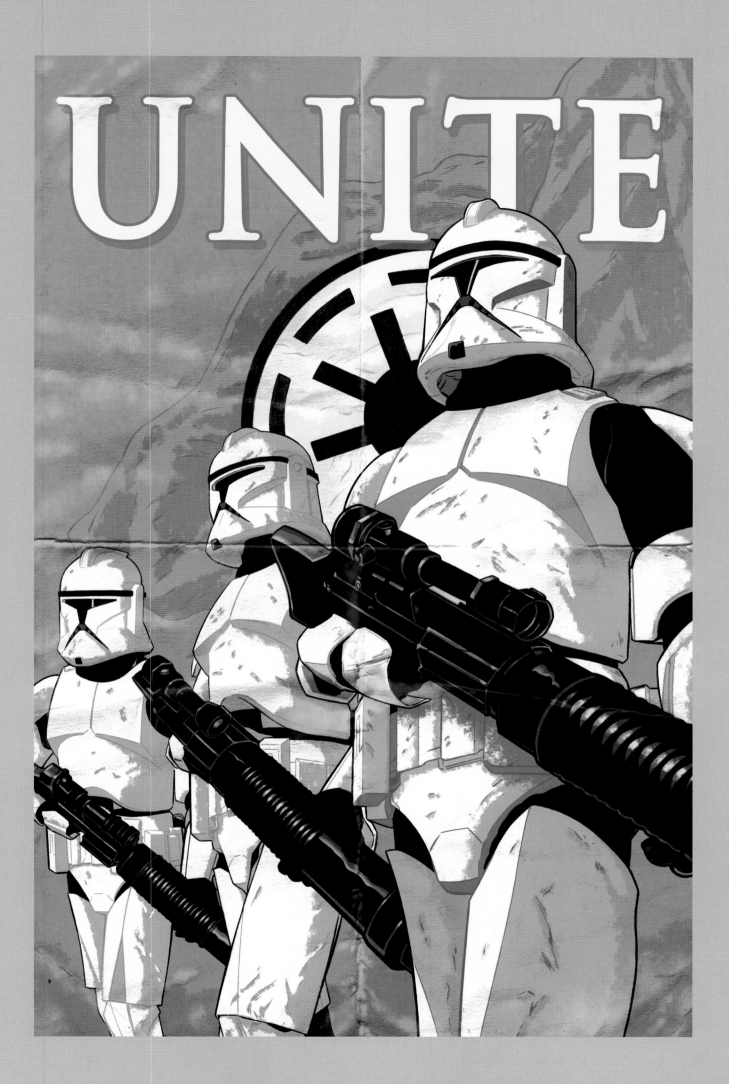

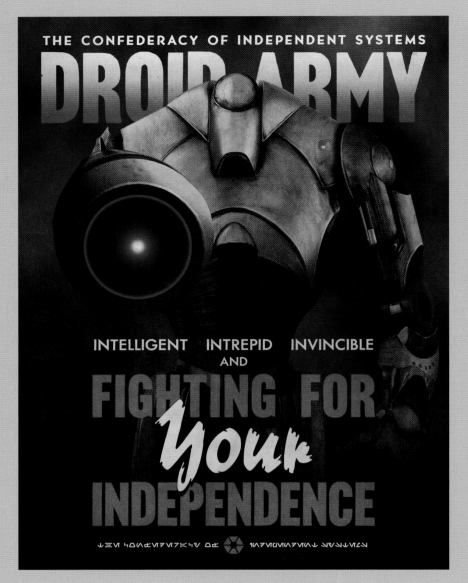

THE CONFEDERACY OF INDEPENDENT SYSTEMS

DROID ARMY

INTELLIGENT   INTREPID   INVINCIBLE
AND

FIGHTING FOR *Your* INDEPENDENCE

◁

FIGHTING FOR YOUR INDEPENDENCE
Q2-B3KO

The galaxy has long had an uneven relationship between organics and mechanicals. History records uprisings and clashes in ancient times as droids became increasingly commonplace in galactic society. It was the Clone Wars that cemented the "droid as an existential threat to biological life" narrative in the minds of the fearful and bigoted. Feeding on this sentiment, Republic propaganda churned out an endless barrage of terrifying images of droid-delivered destruction. In worlds aligned with the Separatist Alliance—or that neighbored Separatist territory—the tone was just the opposite. The Republic was branded as inhumane for weaponizing cloning technology to make *organic* soldiers, while the Confederacy of Independent Systems preserved life by relying on lifeless droids. In either scenario, the droid ended up as the voiceless party—whether casting droids as weapons of protection or offense, no side ever stopped to wonder what the droids wanted.

▷

SUPPORT THE BOYS IN WHITE
Hamma Elad, COMPOR

Early emphasis on the cutting-edge advancements of the Grand Army of the Republic came at the expense of messages based on a relatable humanity. The armored clone troopers projected strength and unity, and it was thought by some in the inner offices of Republic communications bureaus that to expose the faces behind the helmets would weaken this perception. Add to that, Separatist propaganda was describing the clone army as a biological abomination—weaponized embryos carried to artificial term, and trained since "hatching" to be expendable killing machines. The Confederacy instead considered its use of droid military "humane." (Your author points to such confusing debates as proof of the galaxy's inability to fully grasp the ethical implications of the rapidly expanding Clone Wars). Late in the war, attempts to humanize the clones appeared in Republic support posters, appropriating the civilian-coined nickname of "Boys in White." As the Republic began to grow weary of the war, this name would backfire, becoming ammunition in anti-war activist dispatches, pointing to the unsettling fact that these clones were barely thirteen years old.

SUPPORT THE BOYS IN WHITE

DELIVER US FROM JEDI EVIL

Moshenu Phobi

At the start of the Clone Wars, the Jedi were largely kept out of Republic propaganda, with the clone troopers becoming the face of patriotism during the conflict. This was the preference of the Order, which eschewed imagery of heroism or the romanticization of warfare. For the Separatists, however, the use of Jedi in propaganda was not so forbidden.

Anti-Jedi sentiment was more a product of their cultural absence rather than a refutation of anything substantive. Separatist worlds that had experienced lawlessness attributed that to Jedi neglect, a failure of policing. Indeed, the war itself was a failure of the peacekeepers. To these disaffected worlds, the Jedi were just one more symptom of an inattentive Core World. They imagined the Jedi to be cultural elites, or in the case of this piece, a zealous sect of warmongers.

Had the Jedi made more of an effort to engage in the populace, such deadly misunderstandings could have been avoided.

KEEP OUR REPUBLIC SECURE

Yosyro Modoll

The battle droid, super battle droid, and droideka became the default images of droid terror, characterized as ruthless killing machines in Republic illustrations. In the Core Worlds, far from the front lines of the early Clone Wars, a different droid menace was dramatized in imagery targeted at affluent businessbeings and government workers. Personal assistant droids, constructed as idealizations of organic forms, were a common sight in administrative centers. The fear they had been co-opted with spyware to become mechanical eyes and ears for the Separatists was not unfounded. Borderline ribald imagery such as this piece may seem flippant at first, but the haunting silhouette of General Grievous' battle mask is a sobering reminder of the seriousness of security.

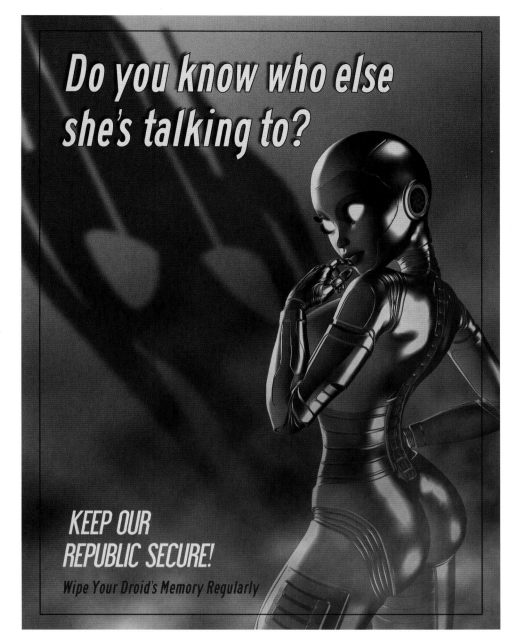

Do you know who else she's talking to?

KEEP OUR REPUBLIC SECURE!

Wipe Your Droid's Memory Regularly

EVIL

HAS ITS EYES ON YOU

EVIL HAS ITS EYES ON YOU
Donclode Onstruss

Grotesque caricatures have long been a regrettable form of propaganda message. Prior to the outbreak of the war, Count Dooku had been frequently described in media reports as "handsome," "patrician," or "dignified" in countenance. Once the war erupted, Republic artwork began to distort portraits of Dooku. In this image, Dooku's features were exaggerated to appear hawk-like, or like a cutting edge sharp to the touch. The specter of General Grievous hovering behind him like some mechanical puppet master served to further strip away any shred of humanity from Dooku. Such is the nature of war; a mere decade earlier, Dooku was the subject of reverent portraiture and sculpture in the Republic, as his departure from the Jedi Order to reclaim his royal title on Serenno was a momentous occasion. But the war transformed him into a ghoul intended to haunt the citizens of the Republic.

DO YOUR PART!
Cosweg Budeesho

With their reliance on mechanical infantry for the bulk of their fighting forces, most Separatist worlds did not have the traditional avenue of military enlistment as an expression of patriotism. However, the battle droids did require construction and service, and Separatist-aligned technician guilds swelled with fresh talent and eagerness as beings opposed to Republic rule joined their ranks. Though much of the droid construction efforts in Separatist and unallied space was undertaken by automated assembly or Geonosian foundries, the rapidly expanding battlefront and escalating need for new soldiers made droid technician one of the most commonly held professions on many Separatist-held worlds.

NEVER TOO YOUNG

TO DO YOUR PART!

THE INTERGALACTIC ASSOCIATION OF AMALGAMATED DROID BUILDERS

UNTITLED
Artist Unknown

As the war slogged on month after bloody month, the citizens of the Republic grew weary of the endless conflict. A rash of underground art began surfacing on cosmopolitan worlds depicting the clone trooper not as a savior, but as death itself. The skull-like face of the Phase I clone trooper armor did a lot of the work for these disgruntled artists, who turned the boys in white into the men in blood red. COMPOR officials fretted about losing the narrative of the brave clone troopers in the hearts and minds of the citizenry. In addition to the violence, the Republic was being bankrupted by the war effort—many essential services were cut off in the name of wartime sacrifice. Had the war not turned during the Outer Rim Sieges, it's possible support for the war effort or confidence in Chancellor Palpatine's leadership may have permanently eroded.

BUY REPUBLIC WAR BONDS
Janyor of Bith

The work of a young graduate of the Cadomai Art Institute enraptured by patriotic fervor, this piece glamorizes the sleek and effective armor of the Grand Army of the Republic. No humanity shines through any crack in the combat gear of these modern soldiers, for to show flesh is to show weakness in the face of a mechanized enemy. The clone soldier became a symbol more powerful than the mortal men beneath the masks. Without using words to express it explicitly, the design of this image suggests that such cutting-edge war technology comes at a price. To the Republic citizens asked to make sacrifices, there was no doubt where their contributions were going: they were funding security in the form of military might.

BUY **REPUBLIC WAR BONDS**

A MESSAGE FROM YOUR REPUBLIC BENEFACTORS

ASSURE OUR VICTORY!

Simeon Densend, Narglatch AirTech Art Department

Expressions of patriotism and civic duty on Republic worlds faced some of the same limitations as those on Confederacy ones. There was no army to join—the Grand Army's ranks were exclusively clone-based. Still, the Republic faithful wished to do their part. A successful war bond program helped fill the Republic war chest, and citizens were asked to make sacrifices. This extended to energy expenditures in such mundane tasks as driving. In the name of rationing, as well as security, civilian skylanes were limited to multi-passenger vessels traveling at specific speed limits. On cosmopolitan worlds like Coruscant, this was an unprecedented sacrifice. For those not able to curb the pace of their modern lifestyle, the fast lane was set aside and accessible only to those willing to pay higher taxes.

BLACK MARKET

Artist Unknown

Increasing demands of the Republic war effort led to shortages in the heart of the Republic, and a society that had grown used to its luxuries now found itself stripped of many essential services. In a bid to secure their borders, many Republic sectors severely limited ports of access. And in this particular ecology of supply and demand, the lifeblood of money and goods finds a way to flow and even things out. Black markets prospered throughout the Republic, despite the best efforts of policing agencies and clone interdiction forces. Addressing such want as irresponsible was a common theme in messages designed to counter the appeal of the black market. Underlining these messages was the moral that helping yourself in this way was helping the enemy, and hurting the war effort.

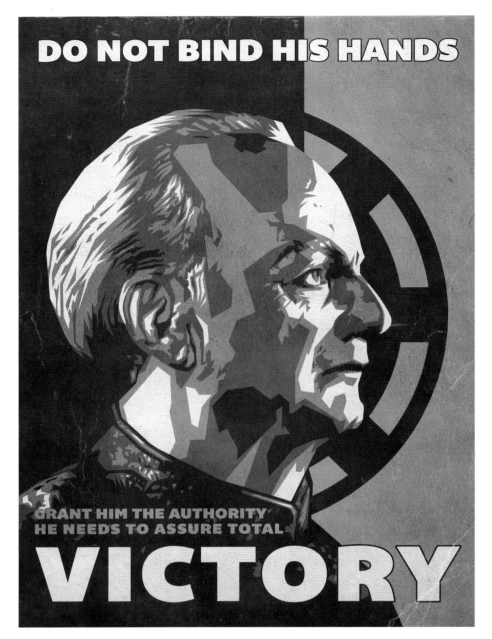

DO NOT BIND HIS HANDS
Venthan Chassu

A shrewd politician, Sheev Palpatine of Naboo was able to maintain the image of a modest Mid Rim senator combating a corrupt and complacent institution despite accruing great authority over that institution. His rise to power was always tempered by a carefully crafted reluctance—his ascent, after all, came about from outpourings of sympathy for his defenseless planet bullied into subjugation by the Trade Federation. He again voiced regret and trepidation at amending the constitution to allow him to extend his term in office, but felt it was needed for the good of the Republic in the face of the Separatist crisis. Palpatine played the role of the beleaguered pragmatist—cutting through well-intentioned checks and balances in the face of extraordinary crisis, making the hard, hand-wringing choices because it was his duty and his destiny. The public loved him for it.

UNTITLED DEATH WATCH PIECE
Veraslayn Kast

The chaos of the Clone Wars inflamed old wounds that had supposedly healed with the passage of time. The independent world of Mandalore is an iconic example of how a planet steadfastly neutral in the conflict between the Republic and the Separatists could nevertheless be radically transformed by the war. Local conflicts between the many Mandalorian clans led to the rise of a New Mandalorian pacifist movement, and for many years, the planet was at peace as it rebuilt in wake of planet-devastating warfare. In the shadows of these efforts, a terrorist splinter group known as the Death Watch was gearing up for an attempted coup. On Mandalorian worlds, recruitment images rendered in the cubist Mandalorian style were secretly distributed at gatherings of anti-pacifism sympathizers. On worlds far from Mandalore, expats were stirred by more realistic renderings of armored Death Watch supercommandos in action—the first time any such warriors were depicted in battle in ages.

LOVE NOT
LASER
CANNONS

JEDI ARE NOT THE GUARDIANS OF PEACE IN THE GALAXY.

DON'T BELIEVE THE LIES.

JUSTICE FOR BABY LUDI

STOP THROWING AWAY LIVES.

STOP CLONING.

RESIST

THE REPUBLIC IS THE PROBLEM. NOT THE SOLUTION.

ASSORTED CHASSISPLASTS
Various Artists

The Clone Wars created a spike in self-published political expression, so much so that in some cases it became impossible to determine which messages were being crafted by government bodies and which were the result of impassioned citizens amplifying or originating their own. It was with no small alarm that the government bureaus of Coruscant saw how quickly propaganda not within their control spread.

A quick, cheap-to-produce form of self-publishing was the chassisplasts, small, colorful adhesives that easily affixed to most surfaces. On speeder-congested worlds like Coruscant, stickers on speeder fairings became the most popular form of political discourse for commuters. A special division of COMPOR was appended to the Coruscant Traffic Violation Bureau to scan holographic records of speeders to account for and track particularly troublesome expressions of anti-Republic messages.

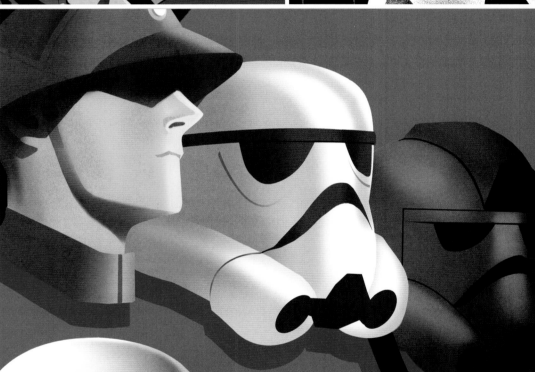

PART III:
BUILDING
THE EMPIRE

A THOUSAND
YEARS OF PEACE

When Emperor Palpatine declared his New Order, he announced that a thousand years of peace would begin that day—his galactic government would rival and perhaps eclipse that of the modern Republic. Citizens hailed Palpatine as a hero. Despite betrayal, injury, and years of exhaustion, the former senator from Naboo had done it. He had united the galaxy.

Among the first acts of the newly christened Emperor was a reshuffling of the political apparatus. The Commission for the Preservation of the Republic (COMPOR), a populist movement of loyalists during the war, was re-formed as the Commission for the Preservation of the New Order (COMPNOR), a useful political tool wielded by newly appointed Imperial advisors with a gift for shaping public sentiment.

In the first few years of the Galactic Empire, civic pride boomed. The clone forces, having done their part, were quietly phased out and replaced by a volunteer army. Ironically, the fervent patriotism of the young produced a more uniform, malleable soldier than the genetic duplication of a single template. This was the height of Imperial military propaganda, where citizens across the Empire were encouraged to enlist in the Imperial Army or Navy. A galaxy-wide military, once believed unthinkable, was now essential to the character of the galaxy.

Military recruitment messages leaned on tradition, honor, and security. They did not need to remind the citizens of the chaos of separatism, nor of the dangers of valuing the whims of the individual against the stability of the state. A citizen's greatest

The shifting front lines of the Clone Wars and the victory of the Republic expanded the reach of Coruscant farther than ever before. The Galactic Empire encompassed distant territories, and evidence of the Imperial war machine could be found on even the most remote worlds.

Following his pronouncement of the Galactic Empire, Emperor Palpatine largely disappeared from public view. Official representatives spoke on his behalf more often than not, carrying out his decrees. It was not until the threat of the Rebellion became tangible that the Emperor emerged on the galactic stage.

potential could be unlocked by serving the military. A stormtrooper or fleet cadet knew his or her purpose.

During this time, the Emperor began to recede from public view. More often than not, crafted holograms or idealized portraitures of Palpatine in his prime became the "face" of the Emperor. The day-to-day governance of the Empire fell to his circle of advisors and military leaders within the Imperial Council. While the military branches of the Empire underwent exponential growth, the civilian trunk of the government followed a carefully crafted template formed by COMPNOR. A series of sub-Commissions began blueprinting what the ideal Imperial citizen would be like and what role he or she would play in the greater glory of the Empire.

The Coalition for Progress, a bureau within the Imperial government that included the Ministry of Information, was essential in shaping the public face of the benevolent Empire (what hindsight reveals to be a calculated deception). A battery of galaxy-wide Sector Monitors—civilian spy agencies—fed the Coalition torrents of information regarding cultural progress within the Empire. Groups within the government would act accordingly where "corrections" were required. SAGEducation (sub-adult group education) would create curricula determined to shape young citizens into patriots. Science groups would guide research and development into military applications. Surveillance agencies would equip the notorious Imperial Security Bureau (ISB) with evidence of disloyalty.

Of particular relevance to this work was the Art Group. This office reported on the suitability of artistic expression within the

Empire and applied inflexible criteria that exemplified its austere tenets. In the early years following the Clone Wars, when Art agents had a particularly scathing report on a piece of art, they affixed a distinctive red holo-label to make clear their critique. This led to the underground term "drawing a scarlet," a laudable achievement aspired to by many counterculture artists chafing under Imperial restrictions. Later, the Art Group was given the authority to call in the Imperial Security Bureau when violations were particularly egregious. The ISB had the ability to make chronically troublesome artists disappear without a trace.

Much of the government communication of this era was strictly transactional. The dissolving of moribund Republic offices and the rise of new Imperial counterparts led to much confusion among citizens of how to best access services. Instructions on how to attain proper documentation, how to present said documentation to security officers, and what the latest measures of galactic security entailed were packaged and transmitted with a crisp, officious tone of duty. Citizens were urged to join Imperial industrial ventures, all ultimately contributing to the growing military might.

Although military history partially records the role Darth Vader played as the Emperor's emissary in the Imperial fleet, he was largely absent from Imperial propaganda. Vader and, by extension, the shadowy Inquisitorius were tools of the Emperor. Their agenda consisted of esoteric spiritual matters of an ancient religion, a brand of spirituality the Emperor ordered his underlings to keep from the public eye. To the uninitiated, it risked appearing too similar to the treacherous Jedi of old.

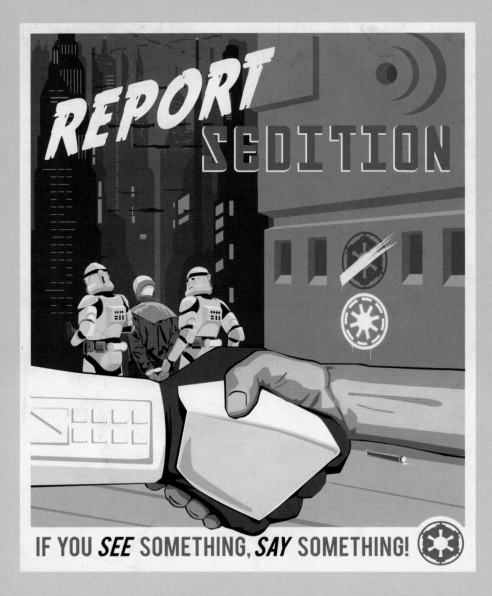

◁

REPORT SEDITION (ORIGINAL VERSION)
Chrigeld Tinnine, COMPNOR

Cooperation and unity are presented in the immediate foreground of this image crafted shortly after the conclusion of the Clone Wars. To counter the war weariness of a public that had begun to question the icon of the clone trooper as savior, officials at the newly rechristened COMPNOR aimed to reclaim the image of the armored soldier as a force for good, a force for local stability. It was a short-lived period in Imperial messaging, as the reformed stormtrooper army would soon be recast in a more authoritative light.

Curiously, this image was not the final released to the public. The Republic cog seen here, below the defaced Imperial symbol, was replaced with the Separatist hex icon upon publication after careful review by COMPNOR, even though that enemy was decisively defeated. Imperial image-smiths did not want create a jarring transition from Republic to Empire in the immediate weeks following the Empire's emergence.

▷

CARRY IDENTIFICATION
Artist Unknown

The Empire swept into power on a wave of goodwill and support from a fatigued populace yearning for safety. This allowed for the acceptance of restrictive and intrusive security measures. The standardization of identification among Imperial officials was an initiative accompanied by a massive communications campaign. Every possible government channel of communications exposed to the public carried reminders to keep identification updated. In this image, the small text carries the warning, "Failure to produce identification on demand is grounds for immediate Imperial adjudication."

Imperial messaging of this era struck a tenuous balance in depicting stormtroopers as heroes and punishers. To be on the right side of Imperial law was the gateway to prosperity and assurance. To brook violations through inattentiveness or worse was to invite the full weight of the Galactic Empire and its reprisals.

STRENGTH & OBEDIENCE
Resinu Santhe-Caltra

Kuat Drive Yards reaped enormous profits by becoming the preeminent shipbuilders of the Imperial Navy. The collusion of industry and military power led to the dagger-shaped capital ships of the Empire becoming the very symbol of galactic might. The admiralty of the Empire pushed this agenda, much to the chagrin of Imperial Starfighter Corps. Historians believe the flaws inherent in the TIE designs were allowed to remain in order to keep the fighter-craft dependent on the capital-scale carrier ships, lest the Star Destroyer lose its position as the symbolic spear point of the Empire.

NOTHING BEATS AN ACADEMY EDUCATION
Artist Unknown

The rise of the Imperial war machine saw a great transformation and homogenization of regional military training institutions. In the time of the Republic, there was no unified military protecting the galaxy. Instead, systems, sectors, and regions protected their own interests by training soldiers to be local defenders at academies of varying scope steeped in tradition. When the Imperial armed forces shifted from clone-based personnel to volunteer citizens, regional governors revamped the historic academies implementing rigidly standardized programs. Gone were the flags, braids, baldrics, swords, and other regalia of tradition. They were replaced with a uniform look embodied by the stormtrooper.

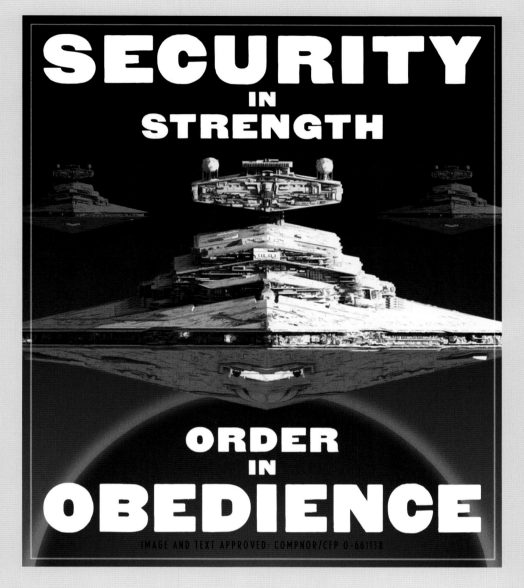

SECURITY IN STRENGTH

ORDER IN OBEDIENCE

IMAGE AND TEXT APPROVED: COMPNOR/CFP O-661138

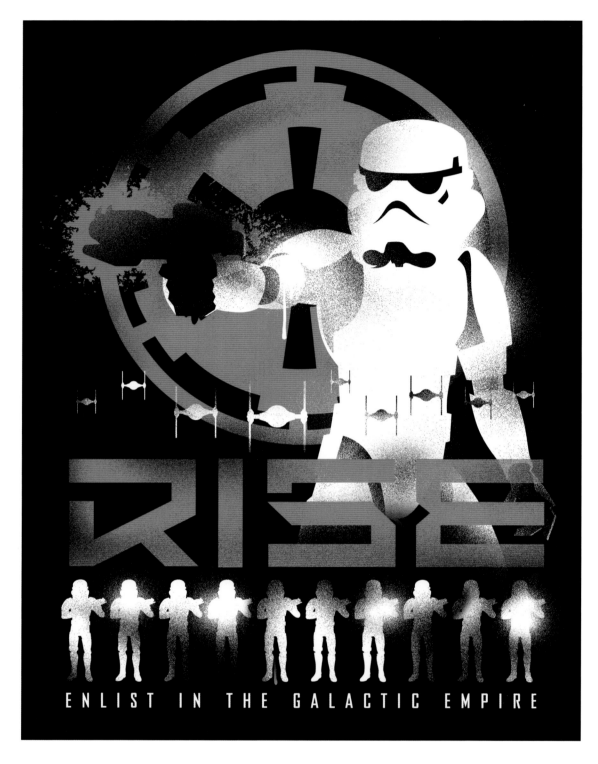

RISE

Coba Dunivee

As the Empire expanded into the Outer Rim, it spread its authority and control over the frontier systems. In doing so, it adopted specific language to appeal to new recruits. The lawlessness of the Outer Rim, a result of Republic indifference, led to the victimization of remote settlers by criminal elements. The Empire offered order and a chance for retribution. To the disaffected youths feeling an unsettling lack of control over their fates, the Empire offered an intoxicating brand of power. There was unity and strength within the Imperial ranks. These messages promised potential fulfillment through military service. The opportunity to not be afraid but rather *instill* fear proved incredibly alluring to an aimless generation.

WE FIGHT, WE WIN

Stassen Bine

After a few years of the helmeted stormtrooper being the anonymous face of Imperial might, the artists of the information ministries began experimenting with using individualized faces to celebrate the armed forces. However, concern from the upper echelons of the military squashed attempts to lionize specific officers, feeling that aggrandizing any one soldier above others would bode ill for morale, and run counter to the notion of Imperial identity through uniformity.

The compromise was a holographic composite of over five thousand faces from the Imperial military rosters. These images immortalized an idealized aggregate. The psychological underpinning of Imperial training, which deemphasized the individual, worked in conjunction with this approach. Imperial servicemembers could look up at such a poster and see themselves, regardless of any physical differences.

IF THE HEADGEAR FITS
Coba Dunivee

With a military expanding to include fresh recruits taken from new member worlds, the Galactic Empire emphasized service and glory. Republic messaging had never been able to capitalize on classic language and icons of military recruitment banners from years past. The Empire, in contrast, took full advantage of the surge of patriotism across the galaxy.

This example is lighter than most, aimed at young recruits in the Outer Rim worlds who would likely be captivated by the sleek designs and modern military technology of the Empire. Pictured here are the head coverings of an Imperial line officer, stormtrooper, TIE fighter pilot, assault driver, scout trooper, and cold assault stormtrooper. Whereas some posters used a singular soldier as a show of strength, this one favored multiple examples to suggest a diverse array of opportunity within the Imperial military.

JOIN
Coba Dunivee, COMPNOR

Imperial propagandists within COMPNOR built upon the symbols and messages carefully engineered during the Clone Wars to accelerate the vast military expansion decreed by the Emperor. This piece resembles the gallant images of clone troopers made popular in the last great war, but adds a new and unprecedented message. For all the hero-building and mythologizing of the clones among the Republic populace, they were always an abstraction in the public's mind, for their ranks were exclusively made up of a single genetic template. Now, a galactic citizen could become that hero once the cloning operations were suspended. Many youths, inspired by clone heroism, longed to fill their armor and do their part directly rather than through the purchase of bonds, the reporting of treason, or the rationing of supplies.

SIENAR FLEET SYSTEMS MURAL

Saespo Choffrey, Sienar Fleet Systems

To meet the demands of the Imperial Navy, defense contractors such as Sienar Fleet Systems expanded their factory operations to worlds across the Empire's frontier. The Outer Rim was a massive source of labor waiting to be exploited. In the farthest reaches of the borderlands, unscrupulous Sienar task-masters created appalling working conditions to meet the unreasonable output quotas of TIE fightercraft and related technologies. Such toil was often masked by depictions of goodwill in enormous murals. When Sienar Fleet Systems arrived on a new world and dominated a population center, such images would accompany them.

This particular example hails from Lothal, a mineral-rich world in a backrocket sector of the Outer Rim. It has undergone updating to reflect the evolving skyline of the Capital City, with the huge factory dome as the civic center. Versions of this mural, with Aurebesh and High Galactic copy executions and other variations, could be found in the outlying neighborhoods and residential districts of the city.

PART IV:
RISE OF THE REBELLION

THE NEW LIGHT OF FREEDOM

Rebellion against the Empire began as a tentative, fragile, and extremely dangerous endeavor. At first, the newborn Empire had the overwhelming goodwill of its populace on its side. The last great war for independence was too costly to repeat again, no matter how well founded the cause. Objection to Imperial policy was tantamount to separatism. Voices were silenced by well-meaning, but shortsighted, allies for the sake of the "greater good."

But as the Empire expanded its influence and grew in power, it became bolder in its expression of control. Far from the insulated Core Worlds, where the affluent grew in wealth, the frontier worlds of the Outer Rim bore the brunt of Imperial expansion. Without the oversight of the Senate, the Empire could exact a far more brutal brand of authority. Worlds that never saw the need to join the Republic were being coerced into inclusion in the Empire by the end of a blaster. Once part of the Empire, they had no choice but to cooperate, sustained by unyielding surveillance, occupied forces, and harsh labor conditions meant to transform frontier resources into Imperial supplies.

The oppressed peoples of the Empire would attempt to spread word of their plight—often through anguished art that starkly illustrated their changing fortunes. But the Empire's agents of censorship drove such displays deep underground.

For years, attempts at open rebellion were fractious, especially in the Outer Rim. Unity was rare, as pockets of resistance were predisposed to suspect potential allies of being competing militias at best, Imperial spies at worst. Despite the best efforts of early organizers such as Senator Bail Organa, Jan Dodonna, Jun Sato, and Hera Syndulla, the Rebellion refused to coalesce into its full potential.

Some rebel-minded allies in the Senate believed that a diplomatic solution could be brokered with the Empire if the right

The architect of the Rebel Alliance, Mon Mothma was a loyalist senator during the Clone Wars, representing her home planet of Chandrila. Alongside such political allies as Bail Organa, Mothma watched the rise of the Galactic Empire with growing concern.

Though history now records the contributions of Luke Skywalker, Leia Organa, and Han Solo to the Galactic Civil War, they were not household names (with the exception of Leia) during the time of the conflict. Very little art features these heroes.

negotiators would step forward. Loose cannons, like Saw Gerrera of Onderon, Cham Syndulla of Ryloth, or the Plasma Devils of Outer Rim, created repeated complications for this political rebellion by striking at nonmilitary targets and causing appalling collateral damage. These violence-minded renegades saw the outbreak of civil war as unavoidable and preferred to bring the fight to the Empire on their own terms.

Mon Mothma of Chandrila had a plan for the Alliance to Restore the Republic—an organization that would serve as civil government and paramilitary force. She just needed to unite the disparate rebel fronts through trust, faith, and a common goal. What diplomacy failed to do, art often accomplished.

The hampering of artistic expression in the time of the Empire hastened rebellious impulses among the subjugated. Cut off from traditional channels, disaffected artists turned the streets of oppressed worlds into their canvases. Some were deeply secretive, never revealing their true identities and letting a clever alias garner accolades and threats. Others were more transparent, by virtue of being in positions of influence, protected by political contacts and seen by millions.

Sabine Wren of Mandalore, Janyor of Bith, Palo Jamabie of Naboo, Furva Keil of Alderaan—the list goes on. These artists began exposing the excesses of the Empire for what they were: tyrannical acts of a draconian regime. Some of these artists, like Jamabie, disappeared at the hand of the Imperial Security Bureau, becoming martyrs for the cause. Others, like Wren, famously took up arms. Still others, like Janyor, continued their artistic rebellion by formally joining the Alliance and broadcasting their message within its command structure.

In the lead-up to the Battle of Yavin, the Rebel Alliance finally galvanized into a cohesive and potent entity to strike an indelible blow with the destruction of the Empire's Death Star superweapon. Within the Alliance's civil government was the plainly labeled Propaganda Bureau. The strategists within this office sought to undo the damage of Imperial messaging, which steadily branded the rebels as lunatics, brigands, and terrorists. The Bureau distributed more than twenty thousand recordings showing Yavin 4 telemetry of the destruction of the Death Star. It encouraged worlds to craft their own messages of rebellion using the imagery as a foundation. The distant depredations of the Empire and remote actions of the Rebellion suddenly became localized for thousands of worlds. The messages of freedom and unity in the face of tyranny began hitting home.

In this way, rebel propaganda became the primary instrument of recruitment. Without an Academy to call its own, the Rebellion counted on its propaganda specialists to disseminate its message within the Imperial Academies, schools, and universities. Frontier worlds that had not been settled and subjugated by the Empire were prime targets for the rebel message.

As the Rebellion escalated its military engagements against the massive Imperial war machine, the work of sympathetic artists made clear its objectives. Their art became rallying points for diverse cultures that would not see eye-to-eye if not for the common threat embodied by the Empire.

For those within the Alliance, Princess Leia was more than just a leader. She was an inspiring symbol. Leading the charge of rebellion since her teenage years, Leia embodied tenacity and courage and appeared in artwork shared only within the rebel ranks.

LIBERTY FOR ALL
Warrchallra (concept); Tavris Bahzel (execution)

An early piece of rebellious art that pre-dates the formal formation of the Alliance to Restore the Republic, this piece has a potent and simple message. With the rise of the Empire came the softening and then outright repeal of laws that criminalized slavery in the galaxy. Exceptions were made by callously reclassifying a number of species as non-sentient. The Wookiees of Kashyyyk bore the significant brunt of this institutionalized xenophobia, as the Empire allowed their use as slave labor. A Wookiee freedom fighter conceived of this piece, though it was later toned down by a Twi'lek illustrator as the original concept was far more graphic and bloody, befitting an outraged Wookiee temperament.

JOIN THE SAGROUP
Pollux Hax (concept); Vanya Sha (execution)

SAGroup—a contraction of Sub-Adult Group—was a rapidly growing brigade of youths fervently loyal to the tenets of the New Order. Indoctrinated at a young age by standardized curricula spread throughout the Core Worlds and beyond, school children were taught that SAGroup was a fast track into the Imperial political arena for those youths who, for whatever reason, elected to forgo military service and early Academy enrollment. Although military imagery was common in SAGroup recruitment images, SAGroup cadets became a different type of servant of the Empire—one that was essential to the administration of the government and its bureaucracy.

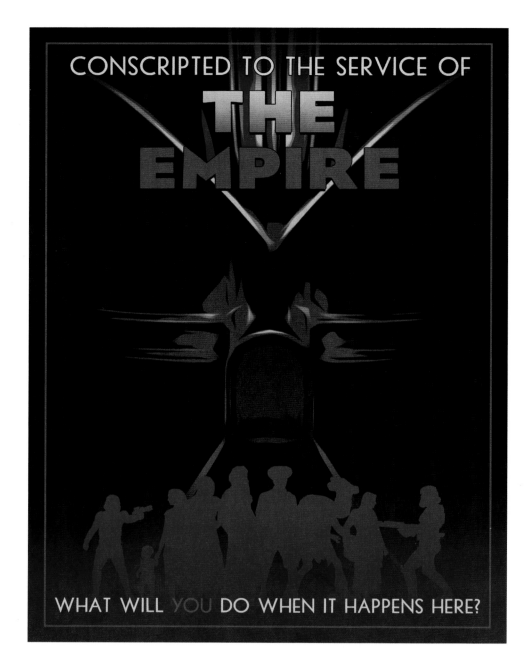

CONSCRIPTED TO THE SERVICE OF **THE EMPIRE**

WHAT WILL YOU DO WHEN IT HAPPENS HERE?

◁
WHAT WILL YOU DO
Cepa Bonshu

While the bulk of Imperial service in the Core Worlds was volunteer based, in time, the pressing needs of Imperial expansion required conscription with steep quotas. It was not just armed-forces service—the Empire began compelling citizens to fulfill its enormous demands for support staff, construction, and other labor. Resistance to the Empire transformed from an abstract political stance of ideals to a more immediate need for freedom. Some of the earliest messages against the Empire came from family members and community groups who had their numbers raided by callous Imperials carrying out a distant bureaucrat's whims.

This rare political work from this early era features Darth Vader as a central design, but it is no accident. The artist hails from Riosa, a world where Darth Vader oversaw the subjugation and the impressment of its population into labor camps.

▷
REBELS ARE TERRORISTS
Artist Unknown

In the early stages of the Rebellion, the hearts and minds of the citizenry proved to be the most powerful battleground. The vast machinery of COMPNOR and Imperial propaganda bureaus could quickly transform a rebel victory into a terrorist strike, complete with inflated casualty reports and manufactured atrocities. Particularly vexing to the nascent Rebellion was a lack of coordination among cells to verify the truth or expose the lies of such claims. Furthermore, there were well-documented incidents where overzealous factions, acting independently of the larger Rebellion, carried out devastating attacks that resulted in civilian deaths. The rebels led by Saw Gerrera were one notorious example, and the Empire capitalized on their indiscriminate actions to paint the entire rebel movement as bloodthirsty monsters.

STAY ON TARGET
Artist Unknown

The effectiveness of small, hyperdrive-equipped snubfighters came as a surprise to the Imperial military, who clung to the Clone Wars doctrine that space superiority was won and held with capital warships. Early strikes by rebel starfighters strained this philosophy, as the lightning attacks by rebel factions split apart Imperial convoys and left even mighty Star Destroyers reeling from pinpoint proton-torpedo volleys. These were not (for the most part) Academy graduates piloting cutting-edge vehicles—these were self-trained fighter jockeys flying outdated craft that had bloodied the nose of Imperial giants.

The Rebel Alliance romanticization of the everybeing fighter pilot truly began after the Battle of Yavin. For his safety, Rebel messagesmiths avoided publicizing Luke Skywalker's name, but the tale of a young Rebel pilot with minimal combat experience who destroyed the Empire's ultimate weapon was too powerful to keep secret for long.

REMEMBER ALDERAAN
Oba Dunimea

It is no small irony that the very instrument with which the Emperor intended to cow the Rebellion galvanized it into the Alliance proper. Prior to the emergence of the Death Star threat, the various rebel factions lacked unity. Some believed a negotiated peace was possible, that the Emperor could be made through political channels to relinquish his powers to the Senate. Others felt civil war was inevitable. As the indelible proof of evil, the Death Star made it clear to the rebel leaders the scale of the threat they faced. Alderaan's destruction spread that message beyond Alliance command. Citizens across the Empire could now clearly see what the Emperor was capable of, and why he had to be stopped.

◁

DEATH IS ALL THEY BRING
Janyor of Bith

The destruction of Alderaan inspired an outpouring of outrage and sympathy from artists across the galaxy. That the government could commit so callous an act of mass slaughter was a terrifying realization. The Empire attempted to explain the destruction as an act of security—Alderaan was revealed to be behind the growing terrorism of the Rebellion, who were on the brink of striking at a vulnerable civilian target. But the general populace did not believe it. Putting aside crippling sorrows, the Rebel Alliance saw an opportunity to strike while the galaxy's eyes were open. Its military succeeded in destroying the Death Star. Its artists kept the threat of the Death Star alive through reminders of the Empire's depravity.

▷

UNTITLED (DEFACED "JOIN")
Sabine Wren (after Coba Dunivee)

Predating the Battle of Yavin, a rash of defaced Imperial placards, posters, and murals appeared, particularly in the loosely patrolled settlements of the Outer Rim. The most recognized practitioner of such underground art was a vandal the Empire simply called "the artist," based in the Lothal sector. Subsequently identified as Sabine Wren of Mandalore, this then-teenaged saboteur used colorful paint bombs as well as traditional explosives to make loud, attention-getting displays meant to undermine the illusion of Imperial indomitability. As part of an early rebel cell led by Hera Syndulla, Wren was able to spread her reputation as a revolutionary force beyond Lothal.

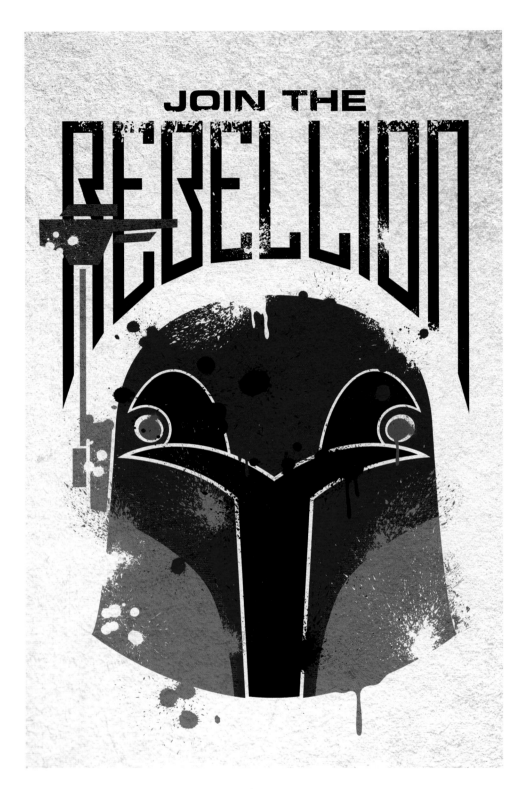

◁

UNTITLED
(JOIN THE REBELLION)
Sabine Wren (Disputed)

Following the spread of Sabine Wren's graffiti, an image bearing a concrete message began to appear on Outer Rim worlds—with an actual call to join the nascent Rebellion and a portrait of Wren's Mandalorian helmet. Wren claimed no direct authorship of the work. The dissemination of the stencils required to create the image was facilitated through pirate comm transmissions and shadow HoloNet data nodes. Though she may not be the actual artist who first defined this image, she clearly inspired its creation and its usage in the years prior to the Battle of Yavin.

▷

UNTITLED (LOOSE LIPS)
Artist Unknown

Found in Imperial military industrial facilities at Kuat, Scarif, and Fondor, this unauthorized and unapproved artwork had a forbidden popularity among Imperial engineers. Playing on the Imperial position of zero tolerance for insubordination and the growing fearsome reputation of the Dark Lord, Darth Vader. The piece is uncharacteristically whimsical (if macabre) for Imperial government art. Some factory managers allowed its presence at classified construction facilities, for the underlying message was valid even if the execution was unorthodox. Legend has it Lord Vader himself tracked down and summarily executed the original artist for a lack of respect; however, this story cannot be verified.

GALACTIC
EMPIRE

HELP END THE REBELLION ENLIST TODAY!

IMPERIAL CAMPAIGN POSTER 34.371.C

Coba Dunivee, COMPNOR

The last known piece by Coba Dunivee, a prolific COMPNOR artist whose art dominated the early years of the Outer Rim Imperial expansion, is an unusual piece. Eschewing the strong, brutalist constructivism of the traditional Imperial propaganda art, this piece is looser, not as defined as earlier works. Some historians speculate this art was a direct response to the growing popularity of Sabine Wren's work, with Dunivee attempting to parrot the urban outsider art approach. If so, such a tactic proved to be Dunivee's undoing, as Grand Moff Tarkin took personal affront to such "sloppy" work and had Dunivee arrested for trumped-up charges of sedition. No records of Dunivee after this event exist and the original artwork files were destroyed.

DECLARATION OF REBELLION

Artist Unknown

This example, found on the world of Ghorman, is one of many independently produced posters excerpting Senator-in-Exile Mon Mothma's stirring words that marked her formal declaration of rebellion against the Empire. Now considered one of the foundational documents of the New Republic, the declaration was made from an undisclosed location and propagated through the HoloNet and other channels in an effort to undo the Imperial efforts to paint the rebellion as the work of bloodthirsty anarchists.

The statement emphasized Emperor Palpatine's crimes against the galaxy and called his rule unconstitutional. It was carefully couched in the language of the law in an effort to legitimize the rebel cause. The rebellion was not a nihilistic engine of destruction. It sought to *build*, and as such, the declaration made clear the rebel alliance's true name: the Alliance to Restore the Republic. Fragments of the Declaration would soon adorn all manner of everyday items and message platforms. In some cases these were directly crafted by the Alliance, but more often they were created by grassroots revolutionaries seeking a unifying message and banner to fight under.

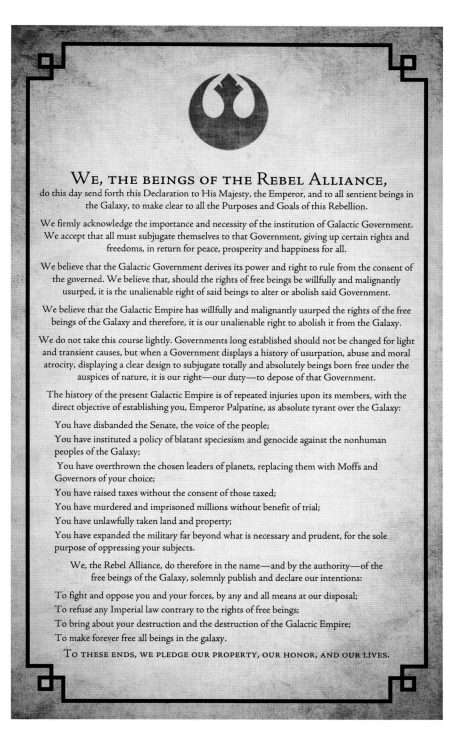

WE, THE BEINGS OF THE REBEL ALLIANCE, do this day send forth this Declaration to His Majesty, the Emperor, and to all sentient beings in the Galaxy, to make clear to all the Purposes and Goals of this Rebellion.

We firmly acknowledge the importance and necessity of the institution of Galactic Government. We accept that all must subjugate themselves to that Government, giving up certain rights and freedoms, in return for peace, prosperity and happiness for all.

We believe that the Galactic Government derives its power and right to rule from the consent of the governed. We believe that, should the rights of free beings be willfully and malignantly usurped, it is the unalienable right of said beings to alter or abolish said Government.

We believe that the Galactic Empire has willfully and malignantly usurped the rights of the free beings of the Galaxy and therefore, it is our unalienable right to abolish it from the Galaxy.

We do not take this course lightly. Governments long established should not be changed for light and transient causes, but when a Government displays a history of usurpation, abuse and moral atrocity, displaying a clear design to subjugate totally and absolutely beings born free under the auspices of nature, it is our right—our duty—to depose of that Government.

The history of the present Galactic Empire is of repeated injuries upon its members, with the direct objective of establishing you, Emperor Palpatine, as absolute tyrant over the Galaxy:

You have disbanded the Senate, the voice of the people;

You have instituted a policy of blatant speciesism and genocide against the nonhuman peoples of the Galaxy;

You have overthrown the chosen leaders of planets, replacing them with Moffs and Governors of your choice;

You have raised taxes without the consent of those taxed;

You have murdered and imprisoned millions without benefit of trial;

You have unlawfully taken land and property;

You have expanded the military far beyond what is necessary and prudent, for the sole purpose of oppressing your subjects.

We, the Rebel Alliance, do therefore in the name—and by the authority—of the free beings of the Galaxy, solemnly publish and declare our intentions:

To fight and oppose you and your forces, by any and all means at our disposal;

To refuse any Imperial law contrary to the rights of free beings;

To bring about your destruction and the destruction of the Galactic Empire;

To make forever free all beings in the galaxy.

TO THESE ENDS, WE PLEDGE OUR PROPERTY, OUR HONOR, AND OUR LIVES.

FLY FOR FREEDOM
Sabine Wren

This art was never intended for recruitment. An illustration done by Sabine Wren, it showcases the flying power of Phoenix Squadron, a hard-hitting contingent of A-wing fighters that raided Imperial supply depots during the early days of the Galactic Civil War. Originally intended as a gift for lead pilot, Hera Syndulla, the artwork caught the eye of Mon Mothma, who thought it exemplified the effectiveness of their fledgling fighter forces. Mothma requested Wren complete it and add a call to action.

Electronic copies of this artwork were propagated through the Imperial flight academies' data networks, intended to show an alternative to Imperial indoctrination that by emphasized the prowess of the TIE-series starfighters. In truth, the fighters, when paired with unimaginative Imperial tactics, were a hindrance and no match for the superior fighting capacity suggested by this artwork.

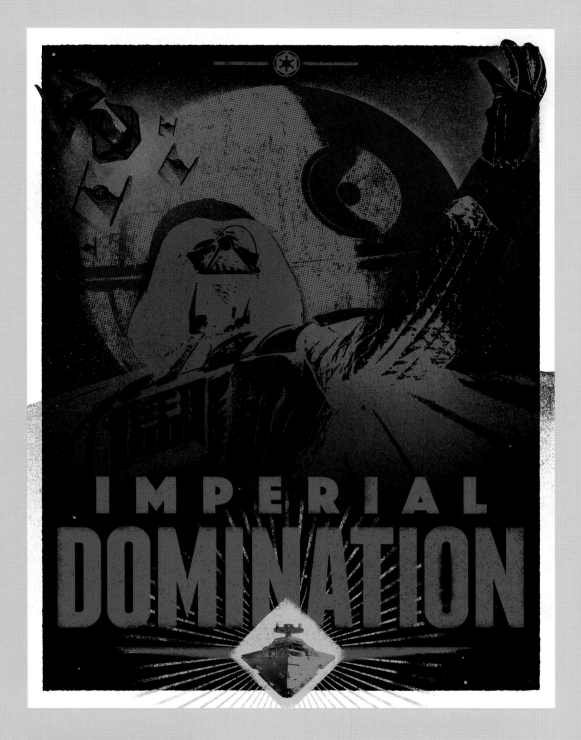

IMPERIAL DOMINATION
Artist Unknown

A curious example reflecting the uncertainty of the times, this piece was discovered in a datapad of a stolen Imperial shuttle about four years after the Battle of Yavin. Examination of the original file could not determine provenance, but Alliance Intelligence strongly believed it to be a work in progress from COMPNOR. It was rare for Darth Vader to be included in any official work. Rarer still for the Death Star to appear.

Without altering the work at all, the Rebel Alliance distributed the image on contested worlds. Rather than have to craft an image declaring the dangers of the Empire, it simply used the Empire's own message as a warning. These are the values of the Imperial military. This is its might. This is the fate of worlds that would resist it. However, the fear struck by the Empire was beginning to fade. Through the efforts of the Alliance, citizens were audience to powerful lessons that the Empire was not invincible.

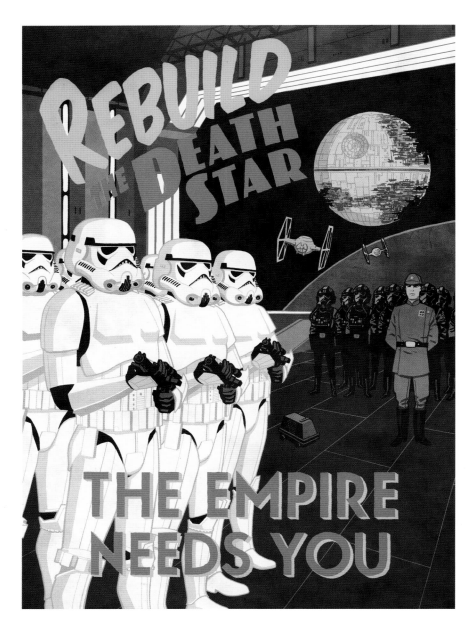

◁

REBUILD THE DEATH STAR
Artist Unknown

This apparently unauthorized poster was found aboard an Imperial materials transport destined for the classified second Death Star. It was recovered by Bothan spies after the said battle station was eliminated by the Rebel Alliance. The first Death Star had been fraught with controversy, thus extant messaging surrounding the second iteration is extremely rare. Some in the Imperial hierarchy, risking treason, openly referred to the overseeing Tarkin Initiative think tank that birthed both battle stations as little more than a military boondoggle.

The first Death Star was supposed to be emblematic of unstoppable Imperial military and technological might, but instead became symbolic of engineering failures, administrative overreach, managerial incompetence, and Imperial hubris. The second Death Star underwent construction in this climate of uncertainty, but nonetheless the Emperor insisted it be completed on time. Supervisor Moff Jerjerrod was less of a loose cannon than administrators past and felt the pressure to please his unforgiving overlords. Perhaps this poster was an anemic attempt to whip up some semblance of patriotism around a project that only raised uncomfortable questions about effectiveness.

▷

EXPOSE, PURSUE, DESTROY
Dasita Lyros, COMPNOR

As open combat between the Rebellion and the Empire ushered the galaxy into a period of civil war, the soldier art that had previously depicted Imperials as sentries and vanguards became more dynamic. Troops were now depicted in action, and the sense of glory infused in this period of illustration evoked some of the more rousing pieces of the Clone Wars. The Imperial aesthetic was uniformly polished, creating an air of artifice that ran counter to the intent of adventurism. The designers (in this case Dasita Lyros of COMPNOR) had never set foot on a battleground. Her models were carefully posed in clean, controlled conditions, a far cry from the chaos of the battlefront.

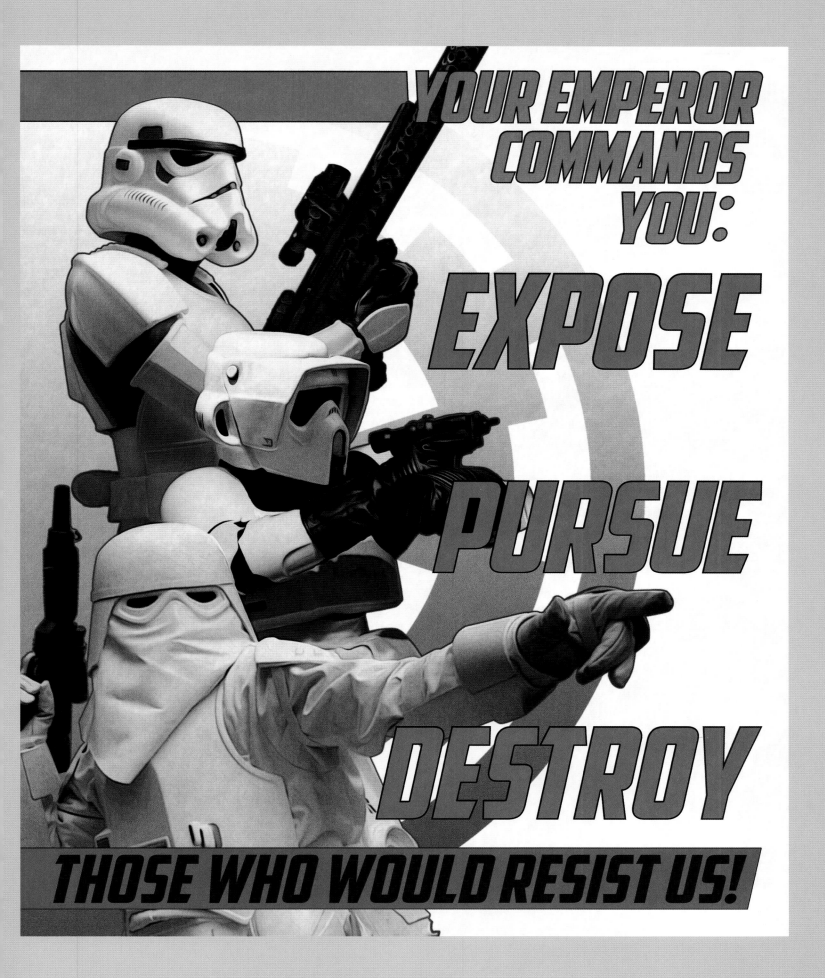

COMPNOR RECRUITMENT
Dasita Lyros, COMPNOR

In the Core Worlds, support for the Galactic Empire was the strongest, as the Emperor's policy benefited the insulated heart of the galaxy the most. However, loyalty purges of government institutions were frequent. COMPNOR orchestrated such displays and rewarded citizens who reported suspicious agitators in their communities. One reward for loyalists was a chance to be featured in the poster art for COMPNOR imagery, to be held up before the Empire as a model citizen. In practice, cronyism kept the actual field of candidates limited to those who already enjoyed a privileged relationship with COMPNOR officials. This piece actually features the artist, Dasita Lyros, along with Captain Edmos Khurgee, who was rumored to be romantically entangled with Lyros.

STAND STRONG
Hobisan Vandron

Prior to the destruction of the Death Star and the dissolution of the Senate, Emperor Palpatine had all but disappeared from public view. When his image was required, often at Empire Day celebrations, official portraiture depicted him instead, and a delegate (such as Grand Vizier Mas Amedda) saying words on his behalf. Such portraiture was invariably of Palpatine in his prime, prior to his disfigurement suffered on the eve of the Empire's founding. After the Empire was shown to be vulnerable by the rebel victory at Yavin, imagery of Palpatine as he truly appeared became more common, in an effort to show strength and resolution.

STAND STRONG

DON'T FAIL THE EMPEROR

UNTITLED
(HE CAN'T DO IT ALONE)

Artist Unknown

This unofficial piece saw popularity in the Core Worlds, particularly on Academy campuses. Though history now has spread awareness of Darth Vader and his role in the Imperial hierarchy, for most of the Galactic Civil War, he was not a public figure in the eyes of the average galactic citizen. Within Imperial military circles, however, his reputation grew—particularly after the destruction of the Death Star, when he was given charge to root out the Rebellion that had scored such a blow against the Empire. Although the Empire frowned upon unapproved messages cluttering its carefully controlled public communications campaign, this image fit within its tolerance levels and was allowed to propagate. Of alarming note is the resurgence of this artwork in First Order territory in recent years.

PART V:

THE NEXT GREAT WAR

AN ORDER RESURGENT

The thousand-year regime did not outlive its founder. The death of Palpatine at the Battle of Endor threw the Galactic Empire into tumult, as the autocracy did not have instructions of succession in the event of such a disaster. Ambitious members of the Imperial Council attempted to grab onto their fiefdoms of power, while distant governors and Imperial military leaders seized what territories they could. Other loyalists tried to uphold Palpatine's vision and considered such power grabs treasonous. Still more Imperials were relieved to be free of their sovereign and sued for peace with the victorious Alliance at their earliest opportunity.

This was a time of chaos. The Empire's expansion stalled, and its aggression turned inward. Governors used their propaganda apparatus to spread tailored messages, which in aggregate were a contradictory and bewildering mess. Some, like Governor Adelhard of the Anoat sector, insisted that the Emperor lived on and that the Rebellion was spreading lies. Others downplayed the threat of the newly emergent New Republic, or refused to name it as such to avoid giving the victors any legitimacy. Some ramped up fear by describing the New Republic as monstrous terrorists, swallowing former Imperial worlds whole with their anarchy.

For the New Republic, it was a crucial time to avoid missteps. Mon Mothma insisted on absolute clarity of message—although she held the position of Chancellor, she made clear it was provisional. This new version of the Republic would undo the overreach of Palpatine and would be a government that was reflective of its members. The communication bureaus of the nascent Republic worked around the chrono to craft inspirational messages of invitation. Mothma aspired to host a Galactic Congress on Chandrila where worlds would vote on how the

New Republic would be structured. The messages of rebirth, empowerment, and self-determination were strong—calculated to win back the former Separatist worlds that had no interest in the *last* Republic, let alone a new one.

Upon its emergence, the First Order deliberately invoked imagery unseen for a generation. The skull-like monochromatic visage of the stormtrooper—a clear evolution of an Imperial design—figured prominently.

The scope and scale of the First Order military operation came as a shock to a complacent New Republic. What were first thought to be local defenses and ceremonial forces proved to be just the tip of a larger invasion force.

The Galactic Concordance, the peace treaty that brought an end to hostility, was at last signed and ratified after the last remnants of the Imperial fleet vanished following the Battle of Jakku. Former Imperial governors were invited to the New Republic, though many of them bore the weight of crushing reparations.

Once the dust of the Galactic Civil War settled, the New Republic was a fraction of the size of the Empire and the Republic that preceded it. Its size was dictated by the egalitarian processes that created it. Many systems opted out of galactic representation, but remained on friendly terms with the galactic government. A Galactic Senate would convene on the capital—a capital that would have no fixed location and would travel to different worlds determined by election.

Over time, the former Imperials reunited as the First Order and coolly inhabited a wing of Republic politics until tensions reached a breaking point. The First Order seceded from the New Republic, a move that was welcome by many in the galactic capital. But others realized that without Republic oversight, the First Order would return to the Empire's draconian ways and ambitious expansion. To counter this specific concern, Leia Organa of Alderaan founded the Resistance, a paramilitary group that probed the neutral space separating the First Order and the Republic for signs of treaty violations.

It was an age of interstellar tensions, of opaque political borders that fostered intrigue and suspicion. The New Republic obsessed over maintaining peace with a light hand, so as not to repeat the errors of the Empire. As part of the provisions of the Galactic Concordance, the New Republic instituted a drastic demilitarization meant to strip the galaxy of any single fighting force capable of vast conquest. New Republic politicians assumed the defeated Imperials would honor this treaty, and in fairness to their naivete, the hunger for peace was palpable across the galaxy. The Resistance tried to warn the Republic that the cost of peace was vigilance, although General Organa was subjected to accusations of fearmongering and saber rattling.

When the First Order's true agenda was exposed in the most spectacular and horrific display of war technology known to history, these arguments evaporated as quickly as the worlds of the Hosnian system. The Republic was burned away in minutes, the result of long-term plotting on the part of the First Order. The minuscule Resistance instantly became the galaxy's only hope. And emerging from the depths of hidden space, the First Order appeared as a fully mechanized military threat.

Once again, war engulfed the galaxy. Once again, the candle of hope guttered in the winds of troop movements. Once again, artists took up their tools to do their part in the next great war.

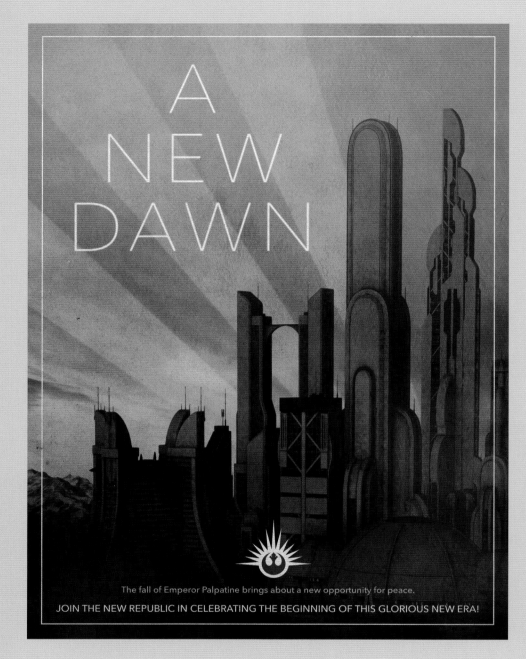

The fall of Emperor Palpatine brings about a new opportunity for peace.

JOIN THE NEW REPUBLIC IN CELEBRATING THE BEGINNING OF THIS GLORIOUS NEW ERA!

◁

A NEW DAWN
Janyor of Bith

At the dawn of the New Republic, Acting Chancellor Mon Mothma commissioned exploratory artworks to inspire a galactic populace newly liberated from Imperial oppression. Mothma rejected iterations that featured Coruscant as the seat of power. In notes carefully transcribed by the artist, she said, "We are not building the Old Republic. That system failed its people, for its failure to listen to their pleas. What we are building will be accountable to its citizens above all." This finished image, inviting new representatives to gather, is instead of the Legislative Commons of Chandrila, the far humbler provisional capital.

▷

ENDOR IS A LIE
Artist Unknown

In a display of cynicism masquerading as unending patriotism, Governor Ecressys of the Velcar sector spread the word of the Emperor's survival. It is doubtful Ecressys believed such claims himself, as contemporary records of his rule unearthed in ISB documents indicated that the governor was no loyalist to Palpatine. He was routinely overheard complaining about the lack of support from the Core, although Ecressys was political enough not to say anything too incriminating.

The narrative of the Emperor's survival was a bid to prop up his own power. Ecressys did not wish to reveal just how vulnerable the Empire truly was, but figured he could hold his territory if he entrenched firmly enough within its borders. Ecressys executed his plan by controlling all communication within the Velcar. He had no endgame other than raiding the treasuries of the worlds under his command. By the time the New Republic arrived at his capital world to bring word of the Galactic Concordance, Ecressys had fled to the Western Reaches with the wealth of hundreds of worlds.

ENDOR IS A LIE

BELIEVE IT
AT YOUR PERIL

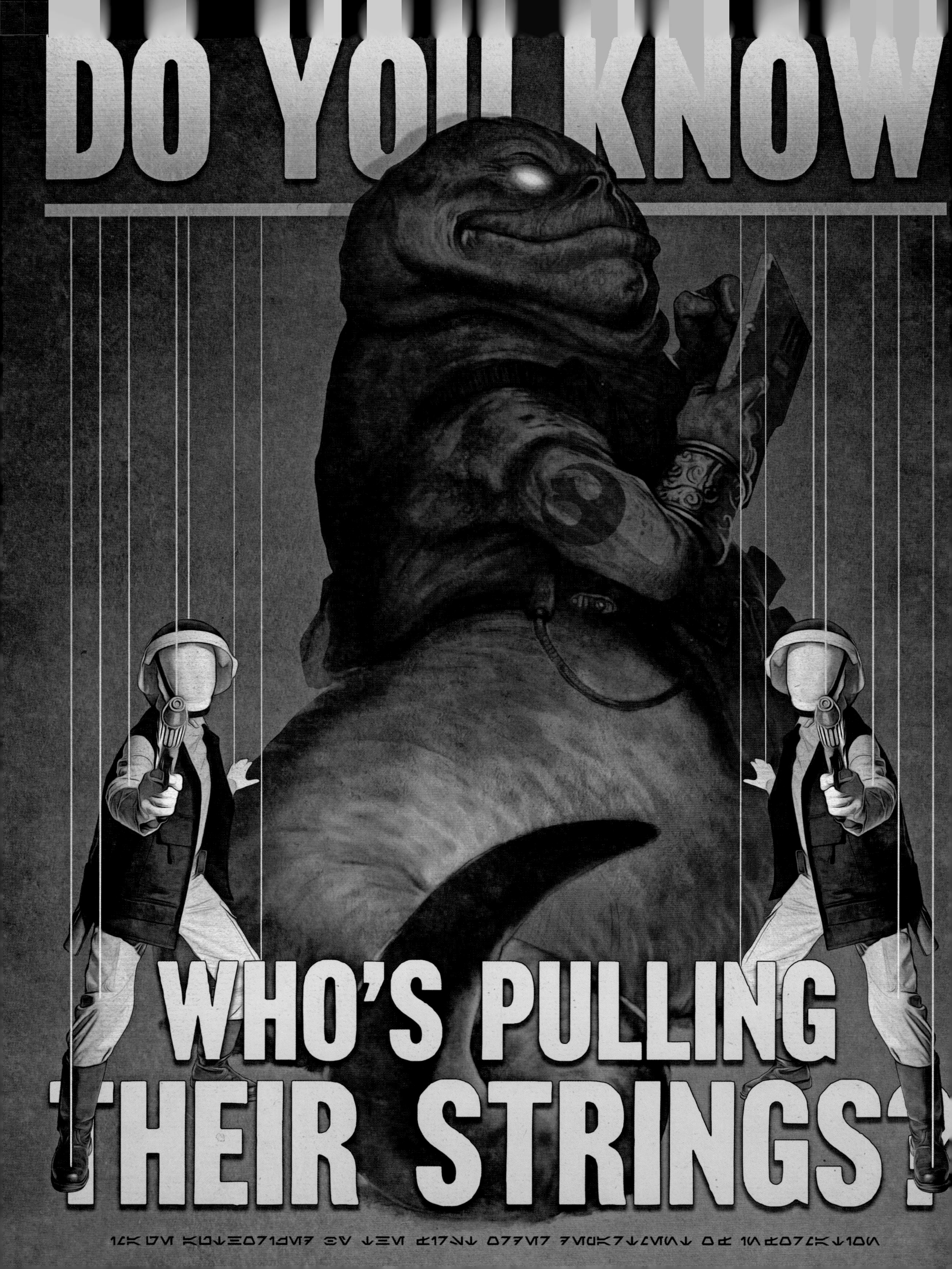
DO YOU KNOW
WHO'S PULLING
THEIR STRINGS?

WHO'S PULLING THE STRINGS?

Ferric Obdur (concept);
Filris Parbert (artist)

Ferric Obdur was the chief information officer in the fragmented Empire commanded by Admiral Rae Sloane. It fell to him to win the hearts and minds of the beleaguered galactic populace, to create imagery and messages for worlds still in the Imperial thrall and in contested space targeted by the New Republic.

With this particular campaign, the goal was to implicate the New Republic as colluding with criminal organizations (a claim, ironically, that could be more readily lobbed at Imperial holdouts). Obdur was reportedly dissatisfied with the exact tone of this piece, saying it relied too much on inference. According to his notes, "We need that connection to be clear, concise: a hard slap to the face. Dose of reality."

YOUR WORLD NEXT

Artist Unknown, Anoat sector

The defeat at Endor radically upended the power structure of the Empire, and a government held together by fear of an unstoppable tyrant quickly splintered. A tide of revolution swept across the galaxy as fast as hyperspace travel and communications allowed. Some, like Governor Adelhard of the Anoat sector, attempted to stem the rise of rebellion by locking down the borders of his sector and maximizing control over his fiefdom. The government directly under his command spread word of the Emperor's survival, even though pirated transmissions of the second Death Star's destruction and the rise of the New Republic found their way through the cracks of his Iron Blockade. Adelhard's agents countered such messages with imagery that recast the Republic as a tide of terrorism to be dreaded.

THE TERRORISTS ARE COMING FOR YOUR WORLD NEXT

JOIN THE TIDE OF VICTORY
Janray Tessime

After the victory at Endor, Leia Organa began to appear more prominently in Alliance (and later, New Republic) propaganda, a role she was
never truly comfortable with during the Galactic Civil War. Once she
came to terms with her status as a symbol, she embraced it, becoming
the voice of the growing New Republic in holographic transmissions
broadcast to contested worlds. In addition to such messages, Leia
appeared in poster art. This piece captures her in an imagined role
of leading a group of SpecForce operatives. While no one contested
that Leia had exceptional combat experience, this particular image
came at a time when Leia had stepped back from the battlefront to
concentrate on matters of politics.

Leia ultimately trusted Evaan Verlaine to manage her image. Leia
herself felt she had much more pressing issues, both personal and
professional, than the approval of likenesses in her portraiture.

REPORT IMPERIAL HOLDOUTS
Artist Unknown

The lengthy process of modifying, agreeing upon, and ultimately
ratifying the Galactic Concordance resulted in a staggered annexation
of former Imperial realms into New Republic territory in the months
following the Battle of Jakku. Some sectors went without a fight and
were eager to throw off the shackles of Imperial rule, while others
proved more stubborn—on battlefields both literal and political.

In the Spirva sector, former governor Callidona Vens was so eager
to prove her allegiance to the New Republic that she unloaded troves
of former Imperial intelligence and instituted a campaign to oust
Imperial sympathizers from within her borders. Her zealousness
actually necessitated tempering from New Republic inspectors, who
feared that Vens was fostering too volatile an atmosphere of para-
noia and hostile condemnation during a time of reconciliation and
reconstruction.

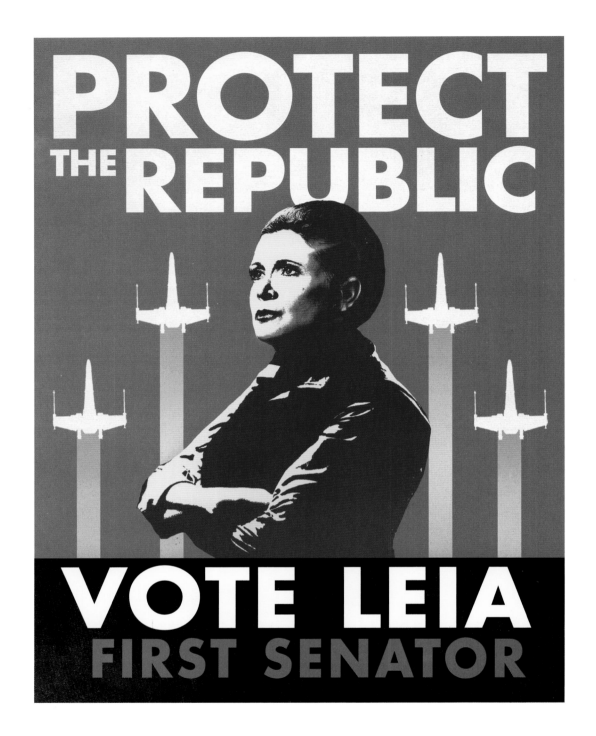

PROTECT THE REPUBLIC

Janray Tessime

Decades of peace within the New Republic led to political fragmentation, as a government designed to resist rule by autocrats instead stagnated under procedural gridlock. The contentious Senate divided into heated bipartisanship. The Centrists—consisting of several former Imperial worlds—wished to create a new position of authority to steer the government. The Populists—those that favored greater autonomy among member worlds—decried the move, but the motion to create the position passed. Strategically, the Populists sought to put their ideal candidate in charge—Princess Leia Organa of Alderaan. As hero of the Rebellion, she would be the best guard against the rise of another Empire. When her scandalous parentage was revealed, her campaign collapsed and precipitated the secession of Centrist worlds.

LEGITIMATE POWER

Artist Unknown

Insight into the First Order remains difficult, as its formation was kept hidden from the eyes of the New Republic by distance and inattention. Although some in the New Republic had, at its start, wished to curtail any spread of Imperial imagery after the Battle of Endor, the new government's dedication to freedom of speech and expression resisted any such attempts at censorship. Public opinion frowned on displays that romanticized the Imperial past, driving it underground. It is in this underground where resentment of the New Republic grew. The emergent First Order claimed the New Republic to be illegitimate, and propagated the belief that the Empire was put into power by the people of the galaxy. Much of their imagery reinforces this.

HOLDING BACK THE CHAOS
Artist Unknown

The territory beyond the Western Reaches was some of the most dangerous in the galaxy, and it was here that the militarized arm of the First Order first blazed through the wilderness like a machete through the thicket. Beyond the well-patrolled borders of the former Empire, lawless pirates and conquering hordes had raided primitive worlds, stitching together a loose patchwork alliance of competing fiefdoms. To secure its presence and test its rejuvenating weapons of war, the First Order turned their forces against these barbarian enclaves. Like the Empire of old, the First Order could legitimately lay claim to being a unifying force of civilization, although the beleaguered populaces of such worlds merely traded one dismal existence for another.

MIGHT IS ALL
Artist Unknown

The era of vast warships that began in the Clone Wars was supposed to end with the defeat of the Empire. The rise of the New Republic initiated a demilitarization effort that decentralized the Imperial army and the navy, and returned the protection of the various regions and sectors to local security forces—bolstered by a smaller New Republic fleet. But for nearly three decades, the hidden forces of the First Order continued the advancement of warships in the Unknown Regions, building upon the storied traditions of naval service. It is little wonder the mighty *Resurgent*-class Star Destroyer figures so prominently in First Order imagery.

WATCHING OVER THE SKIES AND STARS

RESISTANCE

RESISTANCE
Yolo Ziff

The most robust division of the Resistance's minimal military forces was its starfighter units. Following a template established a generation earlier in the Galactic Civil War, the Resistance relied on the effectiveness of well-armed snubfighters launching from hidden bases. There were no concerted recruitment efforts to draw piloting talent from local forces or from the New Republic Starfighter Corps. But the joke among the Resistance pilots was that if Black Leader Poe Dameron posed for a poster, their numbers would skyrocket.

Based on this quip, Resistance pilot Yolo Ziff crafted this faux poster featuring a gallant image of Dameron against a clear sky full of promises, surrounded by the X-wing fighters under his command. Though intended as a prank, this image somehow saw dissemination on the HoloNet and prompted actual interest from would-be Resistance pilots.

The Threat of the First Order is Real! **NEVER FORGET!**

THE MASSACRE AT TUANUL

THE MASSACRE AT TUANUL
Yolo Ziff

A hastily, yet nonetheless expertly created piece, this work was commissioned by General Leia Organa upon Poe Dameron's return from Jakku. His firsthand account of the slaughter of a village at Tuanul—a collective of religious pilgrims eking out a peaceful existence—was concrete proof of the First Order's true colors. The Resistance had been seeking such evidence for some time to make the case to the New Republic and the galaxy at large that the First Order was a threat. Ironically, by the time this piece was finished, it was no longer needed. It was eclipsed by the demonstration of the most powerful superweapon the galaxy had ever seen. When the Starkiller eradicated the planets in the Hosnian system—the center of the New Republic—the Resistance had neither the need to convince the galaxy of the First Order's intentions nor a government to make their case to.

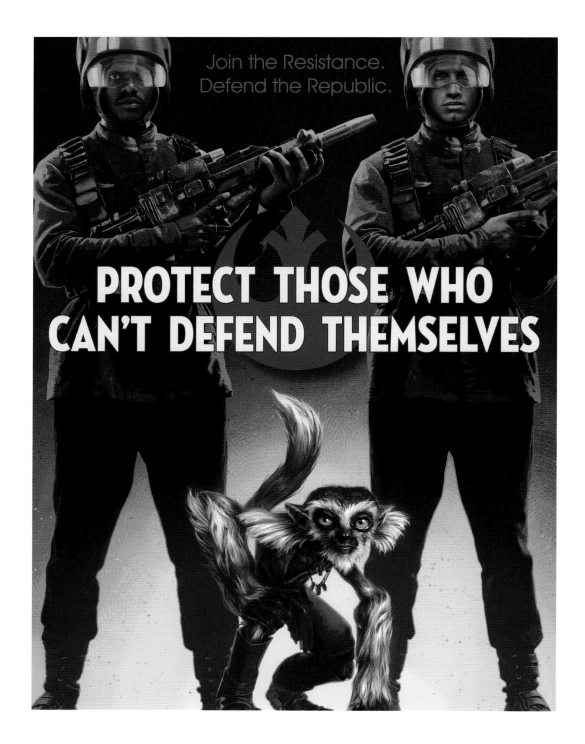

DEFENDERS

Janray Tessime

With the New Republic being chiefly concerned with insular matters, and turning a blind eye to activity beyond its borders, it fell to the paramilitary force known as the Resistance to protect the defenseless. It was a controversial organization, receiving limited funding from sympathetic senators, while also being publicly derided within the Senate for being a destabilizing effort, or worse, an expeditionary arm obeying the commands of a warmonger.

General Leia Organa had little concern over such personal attacks, which was residue from the political fallout that caused her to resign from the Senate. Others deeply loyal to her worked to create images to improve the reputation of the Resistance, illustrating them as heroic guardians of those who the New Republic left behind. That such imagery resembled the propaganda art of the Rebel Alliance was no accident.

WE WILL BEAT THEM AGAIN

Artist Unknown

With its limited resources, the Resistance did not embark on trying to win the hearts and minds of the galaxy. Nonetheless it found sympathizers in the New Republic. There were already allies within various government agencies that believed what General Leia Organa was building. They felt the war with the First Order was inevitable and that the Resistance was the galaxy's only hope.

These specialists were not soldiers and could offer little to the Resistance's armed forces. Instead, they lent their skills and resources by creating and disseminating unauthorized messages to bolster the image of the Resistance from a hopeless ragtag group to an instrument of hope. This sample celebrates the starfighter heroes of the Resistance and deliberately evokes the victories of the past.

ARTISTS
OF THE GALAXY

Information on individual artists within their respective communications offices was not always easy to uncover. Many of the illustrators from the twilight of the Republic have passed on, some peaceably, some as casualties in the wars they were embellishing. The rise of the Empire led to a labyrinthine bureaucracy where records of government employees could be plunged into unfathomable depths should such members be declared treasonous. On the opposite side of the conflict, the Rebel Alliance took pains to protect the identities of its agents, which compounds the difficulty of piecing together their biographies.

Like the soldiers they often supported, these artists did not seek fame. Whenever possible, their identities have been verified by every contact at this author's disposal.

PART I:
THE REPUBLIC

GANAMEY DAVLOTERRA
Art director for *Chrono,* a Core-centric galactic weekly newstack, Davloterra was known throughout the Coruscant publishing houses as a woman of uncompromising political ideals.

NUTE GUNRAY
Viceroy of the Trade Federation, Gunray was censured for his involvement in the blockade and invasion of Naboo, but avoided sentencing. Official accounts record his death by suicide when the Separatist Council saw no victory on the protracted conflict.

RUSH CLOVIS
Former Senator of Scipio and delegate of the InterGalactic Banking Clan, Clovis championed the Muuns's efforts to offer fiscal stability. As a human, Clovis brought Muun issues to the corridors of power. He was killed during a Separatist invasion of Scipio.

TANTAGRU MOTTS-DANEL
A sandscribe from a Tarnab colony on Sriluur, Tantagru Motts-Danel and his Weequay husband, Gojuni Motts-Danel, were a notable couple in the corporate art scene, specializing in holography and abstract art.

PALO JEMABIE
As is common on Naboo, Palo Jemabie was a teenager when he chose to become an artist, abandoning an apprenticeship in politics. Jemabie was sentenced to a labor camp following the rise of the Empire. He would later create artwork for the Rebel Alliance.

NAVEELA BETUINE
A junior Senate official in the chancellery of Finis Valorum, Naveela Betuine was a communications major from Commenor.

DASHIRA DOBEQ
A sculptor and painter from Ryloth, Dobeq exhibited at the Alderaan Academy of Fine Arts, where she found residence in the court of Queen Breha. During the Separatist Crisis, she lent her skills to the Loyalist Committee at the request of Senator Bail Organa.

CODENKA MAFURIAS
Once widely believed to be a Nikto artist in the employ of the Hutt Council, Codenka Mafurias is now assumed to be the alias of an art workshop bankrolled by Marlo the Hutt.

ANSIBELLA DELLU
A student government official from Raxus and critic of Core world politics, Dellu joined the Separatist Parliament, and oversaw the shadowfeed into Republic space during the Clone Wars. She surrendered to the Republic before the war's end, but was declared an enemy of the state with the rise of the Empire.

KAS UNLODOS
An accomplished fine artist from Ukio, unloDos specialized in heritage works that celebrated the agrarian culture of his homeworld. Initially hesitant to enter the political art arena, he was spurred into action by crisis that precipitated the Clone Wars.

MAS AMEDDA
Former Vice Chair of the Republic Senate under Finis Valorum and Sheev Palpatine, Amedda served as Grand Vizier for the entirety of the Galactic Empire, and represented Imperial interests during the signing of the Galactic Concordance.

ANGILAR BOSH
Former art director for a leading Contruum advertising agency, Bosh relocated to Coruscant to pursue government contracts after a lucrative turn freelancing for the Bureau of Ships and Services.

SANTOS BEL-PAK
Poet laureate of Koorivar and professor emeritus at the Lebrasa Argente School for the Arts and Persuasive Sciences, Bel-Pak was renowned for his mixed media work, combining kinetic choreography and procedural with chaos-based rendering techniques.

SANNAB RO
A Xidelphiad entering her fourth protogynic phase after a storied career as a female fine artist, Ro is currently in chrysalis on Level 5121 on Coruscant, and is slated to re-emerge as a male sometime in the next fifteen years.

PART II:
THE CLONE WARS

BYNO DOUBTON
With the influential patronage of Wilhuff Tarkin, Doubton was a fervent Republic loyalist and a founding member of COMPOR. He became a SAGroup instructor during the time of the Empire before retiring to his family estate on Eriadu.

Q2-B3KO
A fifth-degree articulated holographic color separator who was upgraded to first-degree computation status due to a requisition error, Threekayo was recruited by the Droid Gotra after the Clone Wars. She now specializes in disseminating messages of mechanical emancipation.

HAMMA ELAD
A leading light in COMPOR and three-time recipient of the Chancellor Palpatine award for Clarity in Crisis, Elad spent time examining the clone soldiers on Kamino before she perished during a Separatist attack.

MOSHENU PHOBI
An Umbaran working in the printing houses of Plooriod Cluster, Phobi drew censure from the Republic for his habit of sneaking hidden anti-

Republic messages into official communications. Upon termination from a Senate position, Phobi defected to the Separatists.

YOSYRO MODOLL

A Zeltron illustrator famed for her sensual illustrations in semiproscribed holo-periodicals, Modoll plea-bargained an obscenity charge by doing government work.

DONCLODE ONSTRUSS

Independent Holonet Node operator was recruited by COMPOR after his transmissions and postings drew the eye of Senator Orn Free Taa of Ryloth. Onstruss was airlifted out of a Zequardia combat zone and relocated to Coruscant.

COSWEG BUDEESHO

Budeesho was a veteran holographer and cartoonist whose work appeared in material from TriPlanetary Press, Baobab Publishing, the Shafr Center Press, and other small publishing houses. He lived on Ando Prime with his wife, Seeja, and tooka, Yari.

JANYOR OF BITH

See page 9.

SIMEON DENSEND

A repulsorcraft designer who freelanced for Incom, SoroSuub, and Mekuun, and later worked for Narglatch AirTech, Densend relocated along with his family to Coruscant. when Onderon seceded from the Republic.

VENTHAN CHASSU

A prodigy from the SAGroup in COMPOR, Chassu was a fervent loyalist and admirer of Chancellor Palpatine. During the Galactic Civil War, Chassu served in the Imperial Court as a junior advisor. It is believed he fled known space during the Battle of Jakku.

VERASLAYN KAST

A follower of Pre Vizsla during the rise of the Shadow Collective in the Clone Wars, Kast was killed in the civil war that wracked her home planet. Much of her art was destroyed by Imperial supercommandos.

PART III:
BUILDING THE EMPIRE

CHRIGELD TINNINE

An Alderaan-based illustrator, Tinnine volunteered his art to COMPNOR in a display of loyalty. Ultimately pushed out by younger artists, Tinnine retired to Alderaan, where he perished when the Death Star struck.

RESINU SANTHE-CALTRA

An aristocrat married into the powerful Santhe family of Lianna, Santhe-Caltra studied at the Royal Academy of Arts on Atrisia, earning accolades for her work celebrating the Imperial armed forces.

COBA DUNIVEE

An art director and concept illustrator for a Corellian holographic media conglomerate, Dunivee executed thousands of pro-Republic pieces during the Clone Wars, and mentored young propagandists under the Empire. When her art failed to align with the COMPNOR agenda following the rebel outbreaks, Dunivee was arrested for treason and disappeared without a trace.

STASSEN BINE

No record exists for Stassen Bine. It is believed to be a pseudonym that is yet to be identified.

SAESPO CHOFFREY

Cousin to Resinu Santhe-Caltra, Choffrey networked his family relations into a successful illustration career as part of Sienar Fleet Systems. He is retired and living on Garel.

PART IV:
RISE OF THE REBELLION

WARRCHALLRA

A Wookiee wroshyr-wood sculptor from Kachirho, Warrchallra was a veteran of the Clone Wars who lived in exile during the Imperial occupation. He served as part of the Wookiee underground for years and now focuses his efforts on art celebrating his people.

TAVRIS BAHZEL

A Clawdite model and artist known for experimental designs that challenge the notions of species identities, Bahzel spent years following the rise of the Empire helping the Wookiee underground.

POLLUX HAX

For much of the Empire's reign, Hax served as the Minister of Information for COMPNOR. He was the principal state mouthpiece to the Imperial Press Corps.

CEPA BONSHU

After retiring from a long career in communication arts, Cepa Bonshu now teaches at the Ord Canfre Institute for Ethics in Art Criticism.

VANYA SHA

Sha was a self-taught artist who reinforced her natural talent with knowledge cartridges slotted into her AJ^6 borg brain. Her career came to an end when her infocache was breached by rebel-leaning slicers, exposing anti-Imperial sympathies.

SABINE WREN

Once a star pupil at the Imperial Academy of Mandalore, Sabine Wren fled to become a bounty hunter and then joined the early rebellion. A talented artist, she used urban street art—particularly graffiti—to spread messages of revolution.

OBA DUNIMEA

A sculptor, novelist, and composer from Alderaan, Dunimea was one of the loudest critics of the Empire. She was killed by a group of ISB officers tasked with silencing Alderaanian survivors.

DASITA LYROS

A one-time fashion holographer turned COMPNOR art director, Lyros found success glorifying the Imperial military. She was briefly rumored to have had a romantic entanglement with an Imperial officer, but it was ultimately dismissed.

HOBISAN VANDRON

A distant relation to a member of the Imperial Advisory Council, Vandron venerated Palpatine and was one in a generation allowed to paint his portraiture in official works.

PART V:
THE NEXT GREAT WAR

YOLO ZIFF

A talented holographer, digital editor, and illustrator, Ziff is also a starfighter pilot in the Resistance. He flew as part of the X-wing squadron attacked on Starkiller Base.

FERRIC OBDUR

Chief information officer in the fragmented Empire headed by Admiral Rae Sloane, Obdur specialized in campaigns designed to discredit the legitimacy of the New Republic.

FILRIS PARBERT

A war orphan of the Clone Wars, Parbert was raised on Coruscant. While traveling the battlefronts of the Galactic Civil War as a holographer, Parbert's suffered a traumatic injury that left him reliant on cybernetic reconstruction. The injury solidified his views of the rebellion as a chaotic force of destruction.

JANRAY TESSIME

An Alderaanian survivor, Tessime spent much of the Galactic Civil War tending to civilian populations on the safeworld of New Alderaan. Tessime contributed to the rebel and New Republic efforts through her art.

ACKNOWLEDGMENTS

This book is masquerading as a tome that has somehow been transported from a galaxy, far, far away and has fallen into your hands. As such, the true artists behind the works contained within it are, for the purposes of this illusion, hidden behind *Star Wars* monikers and identities. But they are the starting point that made this book possible. This book could not exist without them, and so I extend deep appreciation to them all.

Special thanks to my editor Delia Greve for bringing me aboard this project and entrusting me to run with it, and keeping me on schedule. From Lucasfilm's publishing group, I thank Frank Parisi and Michael Siglain for their continued invitations to add to the *Star Wars* bookshelf. In the Lucasfilm Story Group, I extend much appreciation to Kiri Hart for her support and encouragement.

This book definitely benefits from the advantageous position I have, sitting ringside to *The Force Awakens*, *Star Wars Rebels*, *Rogue One: A Star Wars Story*, and more during development. To the creative teams and leadership behind such projects, I extend my enthusiastic thanks for being so generous with their time and access.

Star Wars Propaganda draws great inspiration from real world examples of wartime art, and lengthy visits to the Imperial War Museum has shaped the ideas and language within these pages.

The greatest source of inspiration, of course, is the mythology created by George Lucas, who set the example that all of us creatively involved in *Star Wars* aspire to.

ABOUT THE AUTHOR

Photo by Joel Aron.

A lifelong *Star Wars* fan and recognized expert on the depth and history of the saga, Pablo Hidalgo started writing professionally on the subject in 1995, penning articles for the original *Star Wars* role-playing game from West End Games. He was one of the first online fans to attempt to tackle cataloging and inventorying the *Star Wars* universe in 1997 with the *Star Wars* Index, a fan encyclopedia he eventually moved offline.

In 2000, he switched careers from being a visual-effects concept artist and digital compositor to a full-time *Star Wars* authority at Lucasfilm, joining the company's online team as a content developer for the official *Star Wars* website. In 2003, he accompanied the Episode III crew as the on-set diarist, reporting daily from Sydney and London during the movie's production and postproduction periods. His close involvement with the making of Episode III netted him a walk-on cameo role in *Revenge of the Sith*.

In 2010, he moved from managing StarWars.com to becoming a Brand Communications Manager for Lucasfilm, ensuring consistency in the expression of the brand across a variety of channels. When Lucasfilm returned to active film production on the *Star Wars* saga under the leadership of Kathleen Kennedy, Hidalgo moved into the Lucasfilm Story Group as a creative executive working on the development of *Star Wars* storytelling across all media, including feature films, animated television, videogames, novels, comic books, and more. As a member of ILMxLAB, he is also helping define storytelling in emerging media like virtual and augmented reality.

In addition to his numerous published *Star Wars* works, he has written books about *G.I. Joe* and *Transformers*. He lives in San Francisco with his wife, Kristen, two cats, and a dog.

Star Wars Propaganda: A History of Perssuasive Art in the Galaxy
© and ™ 2016 Lucasfilm Ltd.

HarperCollins books may be purchased for educational, business, or sales promotional use. For information please e-mail the Special Markets Department at SPsales@harpercollins.com.

First published in 2016 by
Harper Design
An Imprint of HarperCollins *Publishers*
195 Broadway
New York, NY 10007
Tel: (212) 207-7000
Fax: (855) 746-6023
harperdesign@harpercollins.com
www.hc.com

This edition distributed throughout the world by:
HarperCollins *Publishers*
195 Broadway
New York, NY 10007

Produced by becker&mayer! LLC

Library of Congress Control Number: 2016933585

ISBN: 978-0-06-246682-2

First Printing, 2016

Printed and bound in Shenzhen, China

Illustrations and designs by:
Marie Bergeron: p. 39, 44
Scott Biel: p. 100
Rosanna Brockley: p. 6, 18, 20, 26, 50, 51, 82
Cliff Chiang: p. 79, 84, 88
Amy Beth Christenson: p. 62
Joe Corroney: p. 16, 28, 37, 98, 99
Sam Dawson: p. 45, 83
Marko Manev: p. 70, 97, 101, 103
Mark McHaley: p. 49
Ben McLeod: p. 40, 102
Brian Miller: p. 74
Kilian Plunkett: p. 23
Pat Presley: p. 64
Adam Rabalais: p. 73, 75, 87
Brian Rood: p. 93
Eric Tan: p. 60, 63, 77, 78, 80, 92
Steven Thomas: p. 19, 36, 56, 58, 71
Chris Trevas: p. 76, 82, 104, 105, 106, 107
Russell Walks: p. 7, 8, 14, 17, 22, 27, 30, 31, 38, 41, 42, 43, 46, 47, 48, 57, 59, 72, 85, 86, 94, 95, 96
Velvet Engine: p. 61